the Driftwood Diaries

Ava Wilson

the Driftwood Diaries

Ava Wilson

CROOKED RIVER PUBLISHING
TERREBONNE, OREGON

To order, visit our website www.avawilsonauthor.com

Printed in the United States of America at Gorham Printing, Centralia, WA

ISBN 978-0-615-42109-4

For Dan

CONTENTS

The Stone Lamp

June 15, 1950—I managed to build a better shelter today, since the bone-numbing drizzle continues to plague our days and nights. My young companion, Ivan, has a fever, and I suspect he has an infection in the gash on his shin. Before daylight pushed through the canopy of dense trees, I shivered from the damp air, terrified of sounds I cannot identify. Ivan says this area of Kodiak Island is overrun with brown bears, prized by hunters and feared by unprepared sorts like us. When he could still walk all the way to the sandbar where our bush plane abandoned us three days ago, Ivan pointed out plate-sized bear tracks. At first I was afraid of the nothingness here, but now I fear we are not alone. It's unbelievable that just three weeks ago I was cooking and cleaning in my Seattle home. Oddly, I didn't feel any safer there.

At first glance the handwritten page seemed part of an adventure story someone had made up. Sitting on the floor surrounded by several boxes of books, Rosalie Evans, a short, compact woman, pushed one side of her graying brown hair back into a clip, and examined a Kodiak Island, Alaska, picture postcard that marked this page in the rather small journal. The card was dated April 22, 1950, addressed to a Marie Martin in Seattle, and read, "Tom and I will come as soon as the school term ends. I am so worried about you! Why didn't you tell me sooner? I am so sorry about the baby. Your loving sister, Louisa."

Rosalie owns a used book store called Driftwood Books in downtown Portland, Oregon. It is located in the old district, where boutiques, trendy cafés, art galleries and other specialty shops have taken residence behind the weathered stone facades. Portland is a walking and biking city, attracting young professionals who simply like to stroll along flower-bordered sidewalks, absorbing the sights and smells. Rosalie knew that the location was part of the shop's success, but her customers would say her knowledge of rare books was the real key. She often bought inventory at estate auctions, and the particular box she was examining yielded mostly large scientific textbooks. Rosalie almost missed seeing the little journal buried under all the rest. Finding personal items, such as bus passes, bookmarks, homework and letters, among the boxes of books she bought, was common; most were tossed in the wastebasket, or perhaps filed in the bottom drawer of her desk.

The bell over the shop door jingled, and her daughter Penny burst in. In her early thirties, blonde and slim, Penny looked more like her father than she resembled Rosalie. Her career as an emergency room nurse had been put on hold after the birth of her first son. In her arms was their shop mascot, Maggie-the-Cat.

"Is the coffee made? We overslept and I just got the boys to school!" Penny exclaimed.

"You look frazzled. Sit and I'll get you a cup." Rosalie laughed, getting up from her position on the floor. She knew that most mornings at her daughter's house were hectic, nothing new. She stepped around the counter to the alcove that boasted a cushy sofa and coffee bar, provided as a courtesy for their customers.

Penny helped in the shop most mornings, and had her own regular customers. She knew much more than Rosalie about popular science fiction and fantasy series, and had turned the romance section into a thriving paperback exchange. Rosalie's specialty, the rare books, filled the front part of the shop. Her serious collectors were the bread and butter of the shop's success, and they were always anxious to get a call that she had found a certain elusive title.

Just as Rosalie started to show Penny the little journal, a tall, bulky man entered the shop, and headed straight for the coffee pot. Richard collected rare chess books, and checked in about once a week. Seldom did Rosalie find a book on chess that he didn't already have, but Richard would always browse through the stacks, and often made what Penny called a token purchase to compensate for all the coffee he drank.

Putting the journal aside, Penny had the paperback room restocked by 11:30, and stepped next door for two deli-sandwiches. The shop continuously had customers that morning, so Penny only had a chance to read the journal entry marked by the postcard, before she left to pick up her kindergartener. Both women were intrigued by the frantic words written so long ago. Rosalie suggested that they get together in the evening, after the boys were in bed. Penny agreed, gathered up Maggie-the-Cat, and darted to her car. Mid-afternoon the shop traffic slowed as usual, so Rosalie began to thumb through the journal. Inside the front cover, Marie Martin's address was penciled, along with an address for *Ivan's mother*. On closer examination, Rosalie determined that the journal covered just a few months. Resisting the urge to continue reading, she slid it into her bag and vacuumed the carpeted floor before finally locking up Driftwood Books for the day.

During dinner Rosalie briefed her husband, Ray, about the journal and promised she'd tell him all the details later. She arrived at Penny's house early enough to tuck her grandsons into bed, and read them a story about a mouse who wanted a lollipop. It was their favorite book, read so often even five year old Jesse could recite the words.

After Rosalie and Penny curled up on separate ends of the sofa with a shared quilt over their legs, Maggie made a nest between them.

The two women began examining the small journal. It was bound in buttery-beige, soft leather, with beaded designs front and back. Rosalie recognized the designs as similar to the style of Native Americans on the Pacific coast. The unlined pages were held in with three thin leather thongs threaded through punched holes. Daily entries began on March 20, 1950, written in small script, some in ink but mostly in pencil. A number of pages were filled with sketches of plants, animals, and other objects. Some days the entries were very short; some days' entries filled several pages.

Rosalie turned to the first entry and began reading aloud.

March 20, 1950—The postman delivered this unusual little journal today. It's from Louisa for my 26th birthday. She says I should make some sketches in it and jot down anything I feel like saying. Ed must not know about this, just like he doesn't know that I walk to the library on Tuesday and Thursday afternoons. He thinks I am at church bible study. I can't check out books or he might find out, but I can get a lot of reading done in two hours. Ed doesn't like for me to leave the house without him. I can't cut my hair or dress very stylish, since he is jealous of any man noticing me. Over the last two years, his outbursts have become more frequent, and usually end when he hits me. I am so afraid of my husband. He has cut me off from my old friends, and few neighbors will even wave over the fence since Ed is so belligerent. Louisa and Tom moved to Alaska five years ago, where they teach in a remote school. They usually take a steamship to Seattle in July and stop by on their way to visit Tom's family. Ed is so unfriendly, it's usually a stressful time, and I can tell they feel uncomfortable. After a terrible fight with Ed a couple of years ago, he threatened that if I said anything to Louisa about being unhappy, he would make me very sorry. I believe he would kill me if he read what I just wrote.

March 21, 1950—Ed didn't come home after work again yesterday. I just pretended to be asleep when he got home about 2:00 AM. Before he left for work this morning, he slapped me for not having his blue striped shirt ironed. I try so hard to keep him satisfied, but he finds fault in everything I do. A few days ago I fixed a new recipe called salmon croquettes. He threw his plate out the back door, calling it dog food, and made me eat all the pieces on the platter. I threw it all up later.

March 22, 1950—Mildred, the librarian, is so very nice. She recommends books for me, now that she knows what I like to read. I know she wonders why I never check any out. Maybe one day I can tell her.

March 23—Ed takes me grocery shopping on Tuesday evenings and we go to church on Sundays. If the church members only knew that this week I have a black, fist-sized bruise on my upper arm, they'd be shocked. My stomach is upset today. I just looked at the calendar, and realized that I have missed two periods. I've always been irregular, but not like this.

March 24—I still feel under the weather today.

March 25—I cannot bear the news given to me today. I went to the doctor this morning, and he is almost certain I am pregnant. For years I wanted a baby, although Ed never seemed to care. Two years ago, I decided it would be best to not bring a child into this house. I feel so jealous when I see families walking down the street, looking so happy. I never knew Ed would be like this. I got married too quickly, but when Mom and Daddy died in the wreck I was so depressed. When I met Ed a few weeks later, he said he'd take care of me, and seemed to enjoy being a person I could lean on. He insisted on a short engagement, so when we married I really didn't know him. Sometimes I start shaking when I hear Ed's car pull into the driveway. I won't tell him about my doctor visit until the test results come back.

March 26—I had a close call today. Ed took me to Piggly Wiggly after he got home from the dealership. As we were carrying groceries back to the car, I saw Mildred walking in my direction, with a look of recognition on her face. I quickly faked a coughing spell, and started rummaging in my purse for a handkerchief, turning my back to her. I don't know what Ed will do if he finds out I have secrets from him. He left just after we got home, saying he would get something to eat with the guys at the bowling alley. I received a letter from Louisa today, with stories about the children they teach. It sounds exciting to be in such a beautiful place, but I don't think I'd like living so remotely. My big sis isn't feeling well. Says she has terrible cramps now and then. But she will see a specialist when they are in the states this summer.

March 27—Sick all morning! I managed to get supper on the table, but Ed said I looked pale and my hair wasn't done up right.

March 28—I found a receipt in the pocket of Ed's coat that is from Zale's Jewelers. It seems that he bought a birthstone ring for someone whose birthday is in April. Obviously not for me! He must have taken money out of our savings account, so my parents' insurance money is being spent on some girl. But I am afraid to confront him.

March 29—Ed had to work today, usually one of his days off, so I walked to the library. I should have the pregnancy test back on Monday but I'm sure it will be positive. I have heard that some women "take care" of an unwanted pregnancy, but I don't know how to do that safely. If Louisa can help me get away from Ed, I would move anywhere to be safe, but I don't see how I could raise a child on my own. Writing in this journal is so risky, but I found a safe hiding place in the pocket of an old jacket of mine. It hangs in the back of my closet, well hidden.

March 30—Ed took me to a music festival in the park after church. It was a nice day until I noticed he was often glancing over at a pretty blonde girl in the audience.

March 31—My hands are shaking so much, I can barely write. The doctor called this morning to say that the test was positive of course. I decided to walk to the dealership to tell Ed. I just knew he wouldn't blow up with all of his co-workers around. The secretaries at the front desk were at lunch, so I walked into Ed's office. He had his arm draped around the waist of a new girl, the same blonde I saw yesterday. She pulled away quickly, but he just smirked at me, like it didn't matter. After she left the office, I closed the door and told him about the baby. He said nothing about being pleased, or angry. He did say that since I had put on so much weight the last couple of years, no one would notice I was pregnant for a long time.

April 3—I have been miserable these last few days. I envy women who are happy when they are expecting a baby. Sometimes I pretend I am married to a different kind of man, such as Gregory Peck or James Stewart. I am certain they are nice to women and would be so happy to have a baby.

April 12—Two days ago I lost my baby. Ed punched me in the back as I walked out the back door, and I fell hard down the steps. Just a few hours later I knew my pregnancy was over. I told the doctors at the hospital that I tripped. I thought they would ask me about the older bruises on my arms and legs, but they did not. I wonder how many other women go to the hospital with broken bones or bruises caused by their husbands. Ed threatened after one of his fits of rage that I better not leave him, because he has ways of finding me. I will write Louisa again, to tell her about losing the baby. I need her and Tom here; I am so glad they are coming soon.

April 16—I can't stop crying about the baby, even though I didn't really want it. My next door neighbor came over yesterday since she had heard through a nurse friend that I had a miscarriage. She brought a casserole that I am positive Ed won't eat. I didn't dare tell her anything about Ed causing the miscarriage but the look on her face makes me wonder if she saw him push me. I was so blind when I chose to marry Ed. I overheard some women at the bakery talking in hushed voices that even when a woman calls the police after she is beaten, they don't do anything to the husband. It just makes the husband madder, and I sure don't need that. I can make it till Louisa and Tom arrive.

April 20—Ed said I better not think of getting pregnant again, since he doesn't want to be saddled with children. I'm going to try to put off relations with him as long as possible, using the miscarriage as an excuse. My skin crawls when I think of how he reaches for me in bed. I'll have to be careful, since twice before when I told him I didn't feel like it, he ended up forcing me, which seemed to excite him more.

April 21—Ed slapped me so hard last night that my ears rang for an hour. At least he left the house then, and I was asleep when he returned. His violent outbursts are getting worse and worse.

April 23—Ed blew up today when I asked about getting a job. The reason I gave him was to add to our savings so we could buy a house instead of renting. Of course I really want to be prepared to take care of myself when Louisa helps me get away from him. Ed claims that a two-year art student can't get a good job and anyway he wants me at home. I suggested that I could take a class or two to learn other skills, while he was at work. He said he wouldn't stand for me to rub elbows with all those ex-GI's now in college. Ed is very jealous of servicemen. He claims to have a hearing problem, and was rejected by the military during the war. I don't know if I really believe that any more. He seems to hear just fine! I think Ed realizes that he is not the attractive man he used to be. He complains about my weight, but he also likes to eat too much. Beer probably isn't good for the waistline either. I've noticed that his hair is thinning on top, not that he had a lot to begin with.

April 25—I have been thinking about how much I used to enjoy sketching and painting. I haven't painted or drawn anything since we moved into this house three years ago. Digging into boxes stored in the garage out back, I felt so happy handling the brushes and pencils. Since I can't work (yet), I can at least keep my mind off my troubles part of the time. Today I sketched a peach orchard from memory that we drove past last summer. I remember how my parents were so pleased when I told them I wanted to study to be a professional illustrator. They were my own fan club.

April 30—First thing this morning I trimmed my hair just a little, and I hope Ed doesn't notice. It's so long and unstylish. I would like to cut it short like I see many women doing now. I bought some spring material for a new Sunday dress, and will get Mom's sewing machine out in a couple of days. My drawing and painting is actually making me feel better. Today I finished a sketch of the old cathedral in our neighborhood.

May 4—Ed told me he is embarrassed to be seen with me, and I need to lose some weight. Just to make his point, he pinched my thigh so hard I ran into the bathroom to cry. I do eat too much. When Ed is gone in the evenings, I just read and eat, and I pretend that it makes me feel happier.

May 5—I have a split bottom lip, from a hard slap Ed gave me. I think it will heal ok without seeing the doctor for stitches. I wish I had the courage to pick up the broom and hit him over and over and over and over and over.

Rosalie put the journal down beside her on the sofa. Penny said, "Gosh, Mom, this is way depressing."

Rosalie replied, "I know. I just want to scream, *fight back!*"

"Why doesn't she?" Penny asked.

"I suppose after you've been abused for so long, it's hard to think you can do anything about it without taking a chance it might get worse," Rosalie said. "You have to realize this was 1950, when there weren't any women's shelters or social programs to help women in this situation. Everyone turned a blind eye to what went on between husbands and wives."

"Well, I can't see how that entry you first read from the journal, about bears and planes could have anything to do with this woman," Penny asserted. "Want some wine before we continue?" Rosalie declined, and Maggie meowed for a treat from the pantry. Penny took her turn at the journal.

May 10—I spent the morning perched on the upstairs bedroom windowsill. The neighbor's cat was stalking several blue, mountain jays, and I enjoyed watching the drama. The jays made a game of flitting between a puddle on our gravel driveway and the twisted apple tree, driving the cat crazy! I sketched for awhile, and later walked to the library. Mildred told me about a recent novel by Steinbeck called The Wayward Bus, that I might like. Oh, I have been checking books out to bring home! An empty Kotex napkin box is the perfect hiding place. Ed surely won't look there! When I got home from the library I had a postcard from Louisa. She is so sad about the baby, and furious with Ed. She never liked Ed, and is anxious to come help me.

May 13—Ed just grunted when I showed him some of my paintings and sketches. I was hoping he would see that I still have some talent.

May 15—My lip healed up ok, with just a faint white line where the split was. Hopefully it will eventually fade.

May 16—Ed came home from bowling about 2:00 AM, drunk and smelling like Woolworth's perfume. I woke up when he fell across the bed in a heap. After sleeping the rest of the night in the spare bedroom upstairs, I just checked on Ed, and he is still snoring away. I will spend the day finishing my new dress.

May 18—I overheard Ed making fun of me, saying I looked like his mother, not his wife. It hurt so much, I felt as if all the air had been forced out of my chest. I do not understand why he would hunt me down if I left, since he surely doesn't love me.

May 20—Ed said he is tired of hearing about how much I still enjoy my art work. I told him it helped pass the time, and he said I wasn't any good anyway so he threw all my art supplies in the trunk of his car to take to the dump on Saturday. When I begged him to let me keep the things, he cursed and grabbed my elbow so hard it's blue and swollen tonight. What would make a man so mean? Why is he jealous of any attention I might get, when he tells me I am fat and old looking? Years ago, Louisa and I would talk far into the nights about romantic men of our dreams. How could I have been so stupid?

Penny dropped the journal on her lap, sighing "I don't know if I can read this through, Mom".

"Um, we know she leaves Seattle at some point. I'll read it on my own if you don't want to do it, Hon," Rosalie offered.

Penny revealed a half-smile, admitting, "I guess I have to know if she gets rid of the jerk!" With that she picked up the journal, leafing through to find where she left off. Maggie moved to the back of the sofa as the women adjusted their positions, and she appeared to be reading over Penny's shoulder.

May 26—Tom called me today with awful news of Louisa. She has been flown to Anchorage for tests, and most likely surgery. Tom has offered to wire the money for me to fly up to be with her, and Ed surprised all of us by agreeing I could go. I really think he just wants to be single for awhile, but I don't care! Maybe I can figure a way to stay in Alaska and not return to Seattle.

May 27—Ed must have read my mind, because he warned me that if I didn't come right back, he would come get me and I would come to regret it. To make his point, he grabbed my shoulder, and squeezed my collarbone until I thought it would snap. As soon as Louisa recovers, I'm sure she and Tom can help me.

June 1—I have been in Anchorage for three days. Louisa's condition is very serious since X-rays show a tumor in her abdomen, and the doctors will perform surgery in the morning. I can't get Tom to leave her bedside, but the considerate nurses have fixed him a cot in her room. Since Ed would not let me take much money from the savings account, I can't get a room in a hotel, so I sleep on the couch in the waiting room. I just told Tom I wanted to stay close by. He doesn't need to be reminded of my problems. When Louisa is awake, sometimes I talk to her about how much fun we had as girls. She is very quiet, but smiles when I remind her of our high school antics. Her hospital room window looks eastward towards the Chugach Mountains, which are purple in the early dawn. Tom and I sit silently, staring at the peaceful scene, waiting for Louisa to awaken each morning.

June 3—My sweet sister has died. Louisa didn't even survive the surgery. I feel like one of my arms has been chopped off. It is so difficult to think of not getting her wonderful letters, or ever seeing her again. Tom is so grief-stricken and needs my help with arrangements. His elderly parents cannot come, so I will accompany him to Kodiak Island to place her in the village cemetery. She loved that community so much, and had put her heart into their work there. Thank goodness Tom insists on paying all my expenses, so I can do this with him.

June 10—Kodiak Island is 200 miles south of Anchorage, but the flight took only an hour. Transferring to a small plane, we flew over very few villages; the views mostly were of vast bodies of water and empty stretches of wilderness. In less than an hour we were landing in the Seal Point village of Anakalik. Tom says the small aircraft used between villages are called bush planes. They usually carry no more than 3 or 4 passengers, and can land on short runways. Every person in the village turned out for Louisa's funeral, and I was moved by their kind remembrances. Burying Louisa was harder than losing our parents, I think, for I feel very alone and lost. Tom just goes through the motions of each day, barely speaking, but I've tried hard to keep him going. He is finishing out the school term which is over on the 15th and will spend two more weeks here, before leaving to stay the summer with his parents. Today I received a message from Ed reminding me I am expected back soon. My hands shook as I held the paper with the words that had been relayed over radio-phone. I know what he means. If I don't return to Seattle, he will come here and track me down. Having to worry about him popping up sometime in the future, would be worse than going back. I'll figure out a way to be safe, and rid of him. Perhaps I can confide in my neighbor or even Mildred the librarian. Plans have been made for me to fly to Kodiak City in two days, where I can catch a flight to Seattle.

June 11—Over dinner tonight, for the first time Tom asked me if I would be ok by going back to Ed. I lied to take one more burden off of him, saying I had found someone in Seattle to help. He seemed very relieved.

June 14—It is hard to believe what happened since Tom put me on the bush plane bound for Kodiak City. When the plane left the village we had four people on board: the pilot, a doctor on his way to another village for an emergency, and a local teenage boy being sent to a juvenile home in the city. Before arriving at the doctor's destination, the plane's engine started sputtering. Thankfully Mr. Johnson is a very experienced pilot and he managed to glide the plane onto a narrow river sandbar near what is now my campsite. After tinkering on the engine, he declared it was just a loose hose, which he quickly fixed.

Preparing to resume the flight, Mr. Johnson said he couldn't take off with all four of us on the short make-shift runway. It made sense for me to stay behind, but the pilot seemed reluctant to leave the boy with me. The teenager, who is an Alaskan native named Ivan, insisted that the doctor go ahead to his emergency and he promised the pilot he would not give me any trouble. With the boy's help, the two men moved a few supplies, the boy's duffle bag and my small bag to a spot on the river bank. Mr. Johnson said there was a chance he might not make it back before the next morning if the doctor needed to get his patient to the hospital in Kodiak City, or if the weather grounded him. Ivan and I watched the plane successfully lift above the river and trees. I was concerned about being left with the responsibility of the young man, but right away he explained that he wasn't a real criminal, just a problem for his mother. He was being sent to work for the juvenile home for the summer, and besides he knew a lot about being in the wilderness. Two days have passed since the plane left. We realize by now that something must have happened to our pilot, since the weather has been clear. The boy says if Mr. Johnson couldn't get back to us, he would have sent someone else. We keep the campfire built up as a signal, but neither of us has mentioned that we have seen no planes flying over at all. Yesterday Ivan showed me how we could dam up a shallow eddy in the river's edge, where we were to divert some salmon. I must have made quite a picture, wading along the rocks in the seersucker pedal pusher pants I changed into the first evening. The only shoes I brought besides low heeled pumps were ballerina styled slippers, suitable for Seattle sidewalks. Ivan proceeded to kick two large red salmon that were trying to head upstream, over the dam. What a feast we had, roasting one on a rock near the campfire. Besides being abandoned and not sure of our rescue, Ivan put a long gash in his leg the first evening we were here, when he was using the hatchet to cut firewood. Ivan claims the hatchet bounced off a knot, trying to assure me that he is not careless. I have tried to keep it clean, heating water in the only pan left for our use. We have discussed our predicament, and if no one comes by the time his leg is better, we will follow the river downstream, hoping to reach the coastline and perhaps signal a boat or plane. The mosquitoes are so thick we have to hover around the campfire, enveloped in smoke, to get some relief. I put on a pair of nylons to protect my legs, tying some string around the pant cuffs just below the knees. I am so scared. I cannot look into the forest without overwhelming my senses trying to absorb it all: the sights, sounds, and smells are too unfamiliar to accept.

Rosalie and Penny looked at each other across the knee-humps under their quilt. "It's absolutely unbelievable!" Rosalie exclaimed. "I am so tempted to skip some pages, to see when they are rescued. How did this little book get to Oregon?"

"Oh, Mom, here is the entry that was marked by the postcard where she is worried about bears," Penny announced.

After a bathroom break, the two women made a small pot of coffee, and Rosalie took her turn to read. Maggie moved to the ottoman, stretching out her full length before retracting into a headless furry lump.

June 15, 1950—Today I managed to build a better shelter, since the bone-numbing drizzle continues to plague our days and nights. My young companion, Ivan, has a fever, and I suspect he has an infection in the gash on his shin. Before daylight pushed through the canopy of dense trees, I shivered from the damp air, terrified of sounds I cannot identify. Ivan says this area of Kodiak Island is overrun with brown bears, prized by hunters and feared by unprepared sorts like us. When he could still walk all the way to the sandbar where our bush plane abandoned us three days ago, Ivan pointed out plate-sized bear tracks. At first I was afraid of the nothingness here, but now I fear we are not alone. It's unbelievable that just three weeks ago I was cooking and cleaning in my Seattle home. Oddly, I didn't feel any safer there.

June 16—Without Ivan, I would have already perished in this wilderness. Thank goodness he has spent all of his life in the small bush community, which is made up of mostly Russian-Aleut native people. Ivan's mother is native Alaskan, and his father was a Russian-Aleut commercial fisherman, but he left the family before Ivan reached school age. I have no idea what to do in this remote place, but I just try to show Ivan I am confident in his knowledge and skills. As the days have progressed, we have had to depend more and more on my following his directions, rather than Ivan doing the actual work. This morning, about 3:00 AM, in the damp Alaskan twilight, I walked to the river to get some water. Ivan had awakened with a fierce thirst, and his wound has become terribly festered. The aspirin I found in my purse doesn't help with the pain, he says. I don't think Ivan complains as much as I would in the same condition. Just as I got to the river, there was a thrashing sound on the opposite bank, and I saw the rear of a buffalo-sized animal disappear into the willows. I dipped the water quickly and ran back to camp. Ivan said I had just spotted my first brown bear, the fiercest animal in North America. He also says we have to be more careful with any food in our camp. That will not be a problem much longer, since we have only a couple of cans left from the box of supplies. It seems that I am taking off some of the weight that Ed complained about! For supper tonight I boiled a hunk of salmon in the one cooking pot, so Ivan could have some broth. His stomach can't hold solids down, but he claims he feels better. He only says that for my benefit, but I know his fever hasn't gone down all day. We talked late into the night about our families. He regrets giving his mother so much trouble, and he wants to see her to say he will do better. I told him that mothers know their sons are basically good men, and he will have the rest of his life to prove it to her. I am beginning to worry that our position is too well hidden along the river to be spotted by a plane. The river is bordered by tall trees, thicker across the river from us. On our side the land slopes up to a treeless ridge. I feel that our campfire smoke doesn't even leave the rocky bank of the river. Ivan is in no shape to walk, and I don't know what to do.

June 18—For two days it never stopped raining and blowing. I had to keep repositioning the one small tarp we have, over the open side of our shelter. The first day we were here, Ivan cut some spruce boughs and leaned them up against a huge tree, so we could crawl beneath the tepee-like structure. It was really too small for the two of us to stretch out at the same time, so a few days later I found where two large boulders nearer the river sit about five feet apart, one about five feet high and the other about a foot shorter. By placing the tree boughs across the top and covering them with lots of smaller branches and moss, it sheds some of the rain. I blocked one end with small, rotten chunks of trees and bark, and our supply box. I built the campfire a few feet in front of the other opening. Our small tarp is used to keep the rain from blowing into our shelter. Since we have only one old army surplus sleeping bag, we use that for our mattress and cover up with the extra clothes from Ivan's duffel bag. My thin clothes proved to be no use at all, so Ivan gave me a pair of his Levis which I can't quite zip up. I burned my useless ballerina slippers when Ivan gave me his extra pair of tennis shoes. This afternoon after the rain finally stopped, we heard the faint drone of an airplane, and I frantically piled brush on our smoldering campfire, hoping to signal the pilot. The sound faded away. I was devastated, but tried to convince Ivan the plane would most certainly be back.

June 19—This morning the sun beamed through the trees in insect laden streamers. After feeding Ivan some broth, I stretched out on the warmed gravel, and a feeling of déjà vu gave me goose bumps. With my eyes closed I could almost believe my sister was lying beside me, waiting for Mother to call us back to the little cabin our family leased one August so long ago. Ivan interrupted my daydream, asking for a drink. I am so afraid that neither Ivan nor I will be found alive on this riverbank. I have written my name and address inside the cover of this journal. I can't bear to think that no one would ever know what really happened to us. The mosquitos are driving us mad. Even in the little shelter, we have to keep covered up, not exposing any skin. I use one of my blouses to wrap around my head, protecting the back of my neck, tying the sleeves under my chin. We have had at least two bears prowling closer to our camp the last three days. At night I can only doze since the campfire in front of our shelter has to be kept blazing. Ivan claims it is our best defense.

June 20—It's clear that Ivan's leg is not going to improve without medical attention. The flesh around the wound is red and yellow with pus. I have cleaned it every day with warm water, but the infection is spreading. A red streak has spread from the infected area, up to his knee, which is swollen and hot. Ivan is often delirious from the pain and he has told me many times to leave him, and follow the river to look for someone to rescue me. I feel so helpless! He insisted that I make a note of his mother's name and address so I, or whoever finds this journal, can contact her and tell her what happened to him. More than anything, I want his mother to know that I consider Ivan a hero. Without him I would have already perished from hunger or gone mad with loneliness and fear. Why isn't someone looking for us?

June 21—Darkness lasts just a short time in the Alaskan summer nights. Tonight when it did finally become dark beyond the flickering campfire, I could hear one or perhaps two bears moving through the brush near our shelter. When they rumble warnings to each other, I want to scream. Or faint! I feel totally vulnerable and would be hysterical with fear if I didn't have to maintain a brave face for the boy. I sang silly melodies to him far into the night, which did more to quiet my nerves than relieve his suffering. I can't allow myself to sleep, afraid to let my guard down and let the fires go out. The excess fat that Ed complained about is melting away. I must look like a war refugee, hair matted with insects and dirt, sooty all over. I think about food all the time, but Ivan claims he isn't hungry anymore. There is nothing left in the supply box, so the salmon in the river is about all we have to eat and I am glad to have it! Ivan told me how to gather the uncurled shoots of fiddlehead ferns. He said to scrub the brown papery covering off and boil them. The resulting vegetable is much like a skinny, leafy, asparagus. It is too early in the summer for berries to ripen, but the green nubs covering the bushes along the riverbank indicate there will a big crop in another month. Ivan pointed out the salmonberry bushes, which he said are like huge raspberries, and I wonder if I will still be here when they ripen. Oh, please, someone come help us!

June 22—We were awakened by a terrifying commotion. Two bruins of massive sizes, one dark brown with many battle scars and the other a younger, smaller bear with bronze coloring, were fighting in the river not far from camp. The "old man" finally ran off the young one. I stayed inside the shelter with Ivan for a long time, before creeping out. I have to walk up the riverbank farther from camp, to gather dry firewood. There are deep ruts worn through the grass that are evidently made by the bears, as very often I have to step over huge piles of bear droppings. Ivan has warned me to make lots of noise because he says if a bear hears me coming, most of the time it will voluntarily avoid contact. Still, I will admit I am petrified to the point of visibly shaking. It occurred to me that this fear of expecting the worst to happen is much like my fear of Ed coming through the door at home. Before I had a chance to think anymore about it, I used a pocketknife to saw off a full two feet of my filthy hair. It is now about ear lobe length and feels great! Ed will be so angry.

June 23—I am beginning to doubt my decision to stay with Ivan, waiting for rescue when we realized he could not walk out. I wish I had paid more attention to the terrain as we flew out of the village to the doctor's destination. I don't have any idea of how far we are from the coast or even which direction we were headed. The pilot flew over many islands, lakes, and bays before he had to land, and by then we were skimming the treetops on endless miles of forest. I tried to question Ivan about our location, but he seems disoriented and I couldn't make sense of his ramblings. If I could get up on the ridge above us and build a large fire, it might attract help. But right now I cannot leave Ivan.

June 24—Last night was a sleepless one again. The bears were so close to camp I had to build a very large bonfire. I wonder if the bears are attracted to the smell coming from Ivan's leg. He drifted in and out of consciousness all day, and when he was awake at one point, he talked about a trip he and his mother took to Seattle. I cried for him after he went back to sleep, thinking of how his face lit up when telling me about the trip. I so desperately want to survive this, and watch him tell his family about this adventure. His mother must be sick with worry. I wonder how Ed feels.

June 28—A bittersweet miracle! We were found on the morning of the 25th, but my young friend has not survived. I was awakened by the crunching of gravel underfoot that morning, and realized in horror that a large animal was walking nearby. The sound slowly came closer and closer to the shelter, and I hovered over Ivan to feebly protect him. I was actually frozen in fear, expecting a nine foot tall snarling bear to rip off the tarp door. The sound stopped, and just as I felt a scream building in my throat, a voice said *Hello, the tent!* I clambered out of the shelter to collapse into surprised arms! A man who has a camp about four miles away, saw our campfire smoke when hiking along the ridge yesterday, and assumed it was a bear hunter's camp. Thinking it over during the night, he realized he hadn't heard any rifle shots and decided to investigate. Thank goodness he did! He made a stretcher for Ivan, and I helped as much as I could to get Ivan up to the ridge. When it became too steep near the top, the young man hefted Ivan up over his shoulder, and carried him the rest of the way to his cabin, which is situated near a small lake. Dan is an archaeologist excavating an ancient site by the lake. He told me that there is a guide's lodge located on a bay about 2 days walk east from his cabin that has a radio where he could call for help. He had planned to leave the next morning, but Ivan never awakened after arriving at the cabin, and died in the early hours of June 27th. Dan said he must have had blood poisoning. I had not slept for over 36 hours when this happened, and collapsed with grief, sleeping for almost another day. I had nightmares which kept Dan awake too. Each time I woke from dreaming of bears and Ivan, he was right there telling me everything was alright. When I finally managed to get up, Dan told me he had buried Ivan as a necessity, until he can have a proper burial in the village. He also had sponged the grime from my face, arms and feet. He plans to leave tomorrow morning for the lodge, and arrange for a floatplane to retrieve me, and Ivan's body. While he was packing some gear, Dan said he thought I should prepare myself for another shock. He had a newspaper which had been dropped off with his mail (his occasional contact with the outside world and the plane we heard last week). An article in the paper announced the suspension of the search for more bodies in the plane wreckage found in a bay along the northern Kodiak coastline. The bodies of pilot Bill Johnson and Dr. Larson were found, but the two other passengers were presumed to have been thrown from the plane when the tail section broke away from the fuselage, lost to the sea. Families were notified, so that meant Ivan's mother was already in mourning. As if hit by a lightning bolt, I realized Ed had been notified I am dead!

Penny interrupted the reading with "Aha!"

"She's got a way out now," Rosalie said. Penny nodded but pointed out that it might be harder to disappear than one would think.

June 29—I agonized all night about Dan contacting authorities to let them know I am alive. Finally, I asked him if he could wait about walking to the lodge, and I would explain in a few days. He is such a quiet man, almost stoic. To my relief, he nodded and didn't ask any questions. Is this the way I will be free of Ed? Could I be sure he would never find out? Dan told me I needed to rest and recover from the last two weeks; besides, he was hesitant to leave me alone right now, while he hiked to the lodge. From what he says, there is no real trail, and it would be too difficult for me to walk it with him. This afternoon he hiked back to our campsite by the river and retrieved the rest of our meager belongings. While he was gone, I washed my body more thoroughly. I still can't believe that Ivan is dead. I will always remember his bravery. I know that without him, I would also be dead. I explained more to Dan how Ivan and I came to be abandoned on the riverbank, and why I am in Alaska.

June 30—Today Dan helped me sort through Ivan's duffle bag and we washed clothes that fit me. Just a month ago I would not have fit into the teenager's clothes, but I've probably lost over 20 pounds since leaving home. Ivan's feet were a little larger than mine, but his boots and tennis shoes fit well enough. My host heated some pans of water, helped me wash my hair, and even trimmed it shorter with the little scissors from his first aid kit. I am still a bit shaky, but Dan keeps plying me with soups and his homemade bread. The newspaper article about the plane crash had published Ivan's date and place of birth, so we fashioned a headstone for his temporary grave. The article also gave information about me, adding "Marie Martin was returning from her sister's funeral in Anakalik. She is survived by her husband, Edward, in Seattle."

July 1—This morning Dan left to work at what he calls the "dig", where he is excavating an ancient native site. It is situated about a half mile around the lake from the cabin. Before he left he warned me about wandering too far away. The big brown bears roam the edges of Lost Lake too. I asked him to show me how to light the oil stove so I could fix a proper supper. It was a luxury to not have to worry about what would be available to eat. Dan has an arrangement with the bush flight service to come every five or six weeks with mail pickup and delivery, supplies and messages. This evening, as Dan sat at the table analyzing the specimens he gleaned from the dig, he explained that the university in Fairbanks usually sends a team of two archaeologists to excavate this site to determine who lived here, what they ate, what tools they used, when they left, and why the ancient people were here in the first place. His colleague's wife is expecting a baby later this month, so Dan is working alone this summer, which is his 3rd year at this location. He is very shy about his personal life, but told me he was born in Oregon. His parents moved to Fairbanks in the 1930's where his father operated a dredging machine for a mining company. Dan's father died last year, and his mother lives with Dan's sister in Prineville, Oregon. I asked if he thinks I am wrong for not letting Ivan's mother know right away, what really happened to her son. Dan said he thought Ivan's slow death would be harder to take, but she would want to hear that he most likely saved my life. When I cleared the table after supper, Dan thanked me for the apple pie, saying it was a treat. He claims he isn't a very good cook, but he is a very good eater! The previous week, the flight service had dropped off some slabs of bacon, ham, cheese and eggs, plus fresh produce, which helped break the monotony of canned meats and vegetables. The fresh foods are kept in a box tucked in a tiny, cool, cellar under a trap door in the floor; however, the meats have to be eaten within a couple of weeks. Besides catching a few fish, Dan looks forward to ripened berries at the end of summer. This evening he introduced me to the sauna, or Alaskan *banya*, behind the cabin. In the wooden hut, I ladled water over heated rocks, sweated the dirt out of my pores, and sponged it off. Very refreshing! When he returns from his time in the banya, I'm going to ask him to tell me more about his work here at the archeological site.

Rosalie jumped when her son-in-law, Mark, stuck his head around the door, announcing he was going to bed. "Are you gals going to stay up all night?" he asked, laughing at our serious faces.

Penny replied, "You wouldn't believe this woman's story! We can't stop now!" The expression on Rosalie's face made it clear they were in it until the end. Besides, the women had consumed enough coffee to keep them wide awake most of the night.

July 2—I woke up very early and couldn't go back to sleep since the sun was up already. When I stepped outside and looked towards the lake, I noticed the way the rays of sun peaking over surrounding low hills reflected on the choppy waves. Lost Lake looked like a royal blue blanket, decorated with sparkling sequins. Had there always been so much beauty in the world that I had overlooked? Even the birds and flowers I enjoyed painting in Seattle, seem to pale beside this magical place. Dan soon joined me at the lake's edge and must have read my thoughts. He said he found sights like calmed his thoughts, and I understand that. Chores needed to be done so we teamed up to wash some of his clothes. Washing is always quite a process: heating water, scrubbing on a rub board, heating more water to rinse, and wringing. Dan has a short clothesline near the banya, and since there was a nice breeze today, most of the clothes were dry by late afternoon. Some days when it's overcast or foggy, what you hang out gets wetter instead of drier! We seem to always have socks hanging on a wire over the oil stove. Dan went to the dig this afternoon again, and when he returned he showed me a bone tool he had been working to unearth. While he worked to clean it, I finished making supper. On the kitchen shelf, I found a canned chicken, which was a hit after I de-boned it and added dumplings to the pot. Dan ate two large helpings, then sat back in his chair and asked me if I minded if he smoked his pipe. I really need to decide what to do about letting Ed and the world know I didn't die in the plane crash.

July 3—Today Dan took me to the excavation site, which is nestled into a knoll about fifty feet from the beach. The mosquitoes menaced us at first, so we donned head nets, but by afternoon a breeze helped keep them at bay. Dan says that geological research in the area indicates that years ago the lake was much higher, so there is a "necklace" around it formed by shallow ledges, rotten limbs, rocks and pebbles. He showed me the careful technique of chipping and brushing away soil from bones and occasional artifacts protruding from the trench sides. Soon I was lost in the delicate procedure. The excavation is in the floor of a collapsed dwelling, called a *barabara* (bar-RA-bar-ah.) The native people were still living in barabaras well into the 20th century, but this one is very old. Dan explained that ancient people have lived in this part of Alaska for thousands of years. They constructed these shelters by first digging out a depression in the earth, building up the sides with stones, and making a roof over the whole thing. The roof over this site had collapsed long ago, so the depression was filled with materials used in construction, such as large animal bones, and lengths of tree limbs now rotted into crumbling papery flakes. Like the shelter for Ivan and me, the natives would have plugged the gaps with anything handy to block out the weather. Dan has worked to carefully remove much of the debris, and unearth anything the inhabitants left behind.

July 4—Over supper, we talked about memorable Independence Day celebrations when we were kids. Like me, Dan has fond memories of his childhood. I then asked him about the studio photo of a young woman and baby that sits on his bookshelf. He gave a short reply that it was a picture of his wife and son, but he didn't divulge where they are or their names. I located my soiled purse, and showed him a snapshot of my sister and me with our parents taken about ten years ago. I cleared the table and Dan began drawing some of the artifacts he has found. He documents his finds by sketching likenesses in his notes, in addition to taking some photos as they are unearthed. He was struggling with one, so I asked if I could try; actually I was eager to get my hands on his colored pencils and art pads. I worked on getting the details just right and managed to make it look almost three dimensional. Dan complimented my first try, and I promptly broke down into tears. Poor man, he was at a loss for what to say, not knowing what had happened! I finally dried my tears, and told him my husband had always made fun of my art work, and I had come to believe that I was not very good. Dan looked incredulous, then reached over and patted my hand, saying I did a better job than anyone in his department at the university. I sketched another artifact while he leaned back and smoked his pipe. This man is so thoughtful and actually quite handsome. He is about six feet tall, rather lanky, wears glasses when he's reading, and has one slightly crooked front tooth.

July 5—I am feeling much stronger now, so Dan suggested we walk up to the ridge that overlooks the river valley where he found us. A narrow trail leads up there, obviously used by bears more often than humans. Dan carries his rifle when he leaves the cabin, but has not ever had to use it on an animal during his summers here. He explained that having to shoot one of the big brownies would be a last resort. If a shot isn't placed just right, it's easy to end up with a wounded bear roaming the hills, and that would be very dangerous. According to Dan, a warning shot usually scares them away, but about the worst thing you can do, is get between a sow and her cubs. Like

Ivan taught me, we make a lot of noise walking through the brush and along the animal trails. The area west of the ridge is forested with large spruce trees, but this side is mostly covered with tall grass and alders. The cabin is located on the west end of Lost Lake, which stretches about two miles towards the north-east. We had taken some crackers and cheese for lunch, and found a sunny, grassy slope to rest. Having already told Dan about my trip from Seattle to be with Louisa and Tom, I decided to finally explain why I am hiding the fact that I survived the crash. He listened without comment while I struggled through an abbreviated description of my marriage. I also told him about the baby. Surprisingly, I was more in control of my emotions than I expected. It was as if I were talking about some other woman. Dan was sitting on the ground with his forearms on his knees, and suddenly he rose, walked a few feet to a rocky outcrop, and stared out across the valley. When he turned, his face was flushed, but his voice was steady. He told me that he had noticed a couple of times when he made a fast movement near me, I flinched, and once I started to raise my arm, as if to ward off a blow. I felt sad and mad at the same time; sad for letting Ed cheat me out of six years, and mad for being such a coward. Dan suggested that I not worry about making a decision right now, and instead spend a few weeks thinking through exactly what I will do. Perhaps by the next supply delivery, I will feel brave enough to fly home; or I could ask Dan to keep my secret and let Ivan and myself remain missing forever. As we walked back down the slope, I felt relieved that I shared my dilemma.

July 6—I should describe Dan's little cabin, with its comforts and furnishings. It is about ten by twelve feet, built by a hunting guide in the 1930's. About four years ago the university obtained permission to excavate this site and use the cabin. The log walls are weathered on the outside, but remain a reddish brown indoors. Tar paper covers the roof, layer over layer through the years, with a long piece of tin bent lengthwise over the gable. Steel cables cross over the whole cabin in two places, anchoring it to the ground. Dan says the winter storms coming off Shelikof Strait could easily take off the roof if not tied down. A small oil stove serves for cooking and heating. The oil comes in 5 gallon cans, Dan says, flown in at the beginning of the season. It seems like we use a lot of stove oil, but we do have to boil all of our cooking and drinking water. Two sets of bunks are built into the west and north walls, but Dan uses the top bunks for storage. Dried and canned foods, like milk, beans, noodles, rice, meats, fruits and vegetables are layered on the top bunks. A space is left on top of the canned goods to store extra clothing. Dan offered to hang a blanket over one side of the room, but I told him we could just dress under the covers, or head for the banya out back (a privy is located about 10 feet beyond the banya.) The room is already small so I couldn't see making it seem smaller. We spend most of our time at the scarred and scorched table, working and eating. Later in the evenings, we use the bunks to stretch out on for reading, with the Coleman lantern lighting the room. Dan has a rather nice collection of reading material; many books are for his research, but the shelves also contain a great number of classic novels and popular authors. We've already discovered our mutual enjoyment of James Fennimore Cooper. The cabin has two windows, one beside the door facing the lake; the other window is on the south wall, where the kitchen area is arranged. I've been warned to always look outside before opening the door, in case one of the bears is in the neighborhood. On the south side of the cabin, just around the corner from the door, a rhubarb plant springs up, already very large from taking advantage of the long periods of daylight and moist conditions. It looks like a collection of fairy tale umbrellas, with long ruby-red stalks and hat-sized dark green leaves. I should fix lunch now, since Dan will be back from the dig soon, and I plan to join him there after we eat. Now that I am safe, and not so afraid, I can appreciate the lush and spectacular scenery. The air is so clear, at times I feel almost intoxicated.

July 7—What a wonderful day! We rose early and worked at the site until about one o'clock. The native people who used this site were not living here permanently, according to Dan. Their small villages were usually located along the coastal beaches or bays, and one of the reasons for his research is to find out what brought the natives here. He says that although this site was not a permanent year-round camp, it was used for many years. We sat in the hollowed area, digging and sifting, brushing and gleaning. Dan found a piece of bone that had been formed into a sort of fishing hook, and that was exciting. In the afternoon Dan took me fishing, with rod and reel. He patiently taught me how to cast a lure, and after some effort I managed to catch a trout. I hadn't fished since I was a youngster (unless I count kicking salmon out of the shallows), and then only with a bobber for fish that seem very small now. Dan laughed at how excited I was, but I told him I was just a city girl before being dumped in this wilderness. We baked our catch over coals in the fire pit near the cabin this evening. Sometimes Dan is not very talkative, yet we have discussed some of our favorite books, like Grapes of Wrath and The Good Earth. My roommate surprised me by mentioning that his wife, whom he met when they were students at the college in Fairbanks, introduced him to great novelists. He claims that otherwise he would have stayed mired down in reading only technical publications! He became quiet and spoke no more of his family. I carried water to the banya to clean off some of the day's grime. Dan had stoked up the little wood stove that heated the rocks, so by the time I applied dippers of water, everything was just right. The steam billowed and I am sure my skin was glowing by the time I wobbled away from the little wooden shed. As I approached the cabin, I heard the sweetest sound; violin music was wafting into the night air, accompanied by the sound of waves lapping onshore in the Alaskan evening. When I opened the door, I saw Dan leaning up against his bunk post, fingers flying over the strings as the bow dipped and pointed. When the performance ended, I clapped and he gave an exaggerated bow, with a grin that showed he was pleased at this surprise for me. We talked late into the night about his love of music. He majored in music until he became bewitched by his first archaeological exposure near a friend's cabin outside of Fairbanks. He seems to be so much more than what meets the eye—not a boring academic at all. He is a very interesting man, who has a very lucky wife. For a fleeting moment I thought about how my sister Louisa would enjoy reading about my adventure. I have to believe she already knows.

July 8—Again we spent the day digging, and Dan made such a discovery; he says it's a stone lamp. It's very simple, just an oblong, shallow bowl of stone about eight inches long, decorated with what appears to be a whale's tail etched into the bottom. The ancient people would fill the hollowed area with seal oil or fat, place a wick of twisted grasses in the oil and rest the end in a small notch on one edge. Dan explained that he and the other archaeologist had already established that this site was occupied only by a very ancient group, much earlier than the native people found on the island when the Russians arrived in the 18th century. So far only artifacts from the earlier period have been found at this site, and nothing that was introduced by the Russian culture has been unearthed. Dan said that since the stone lamp was decorated so nicely, it verifies occupation by the older group, since the Koniags of the later period were not so artistic, and their lamps would not usually be so decorated. An anthropologist named Ales Hrdlicka spent several years in the 1920's and 1930's excavating sites all over Kodiak. Most of his discoveries showed continuous use through eons, with layers of Koniag and further down the layers were the pre-Koniag group. Most of these sites were found along the coastlines where the natives subsisted on whales, sea lions and otters. Dan is trying to determine just why this site, so far from the coast, was used by the pre-Koniag people, for what appears to be several centuries. I asked how he has determined the barabara was used so many years ago. He patiently explained that several methods are used, but one good measurement is the layering of volcanic ash. A large eruption across Shelikof Strait almost 1600 years ago laid deep ash across Kodiak Island, which shows up as a thick yellow layer when excavating a trench. The evidence shows the ash fell after this depression was dug. Another dating method is by comparing the types of artifacts found here, to ones found in other sites. A professor at the University of Chicago has just published a paper describing a new method of *radiocarbon dating*. Although its accuracy is only plus or minus about 500 years, it will open up the field of estimating the age of artifacts and sites. I could listen to Dan all day, as he explains details I never even dreamed about. After returning from the site, Dan decided to clean up in the banya, and I started cooking some slices of ham from the hunk in the underground cooler, planning to add diced leftover baked potatoes and onions to steam in the same pan. Suddenly I felt the cabin shudder, and heard a scraping noise along with the cabin movement again. Thinking it was a slight earthquake Dan says is common here, I almost opened the door to step outside, when I remembered his warning of surprise bear encounters. Sure enough, when I looked out the window, a huge brown bear was scratching his backside on the corner of our cabin! He swung his massive head around, and surprised me again by looking directly into my face! Yikes! I reached for the nearest pans to bang together which did just what Dan had told me would happen: Mr. Brownie turned and as I watched from the window, he lumbered down the trail towards the lake. His thick fur was iridescent in the evening sunlight, rippling over his shoulders, reminding me of the wind blowing golden fields of wheat in eastern Washington, so far away. He stopped once to rear up and show off his awesome height, and snuffled the breeze. Quickly plopping to all four paws, he broke into a run faster than a race-horse, toward a distant knoll. Soon Dan returned from the banya, and asked me what the racket was. When I turned to answer, I saw he was grinning. He told me that the first time he had a window-peeper like that, he thought he was a goner, but the big ones are just curious and smell the cooking. In the evening, as I sketched the stone lamp from all angles, Dan played the violin. I hope this becomes an evening ritual.

"Oh, look at this, Penny." Rosalie held the journal out to show the sketch of a gray, oval shaped bowl, less than 2 inches deep in the center. The whale's tail adorned the bottom, and the notch was shown.

Penny observed, "It's actually quite a work of art. Realizing it is so ancient boggles the mind."

July 9—The weather has taken a turn. The sun is gone, and fog is so thick I can see it come through the crack under the door. Fog can be very thick in Seattle, but never like this. It was a good day for Dan to labor over his drawings and artifacts, so I decided to see if I could remember a cake recipe my mother gave to me. She called it "Depression Cake" because it doesn't require milk or eggs. We hoard

Paul's supply of eggs brought in by the delivery plane, so I thought I'd see how this recipe cooks up in the little oil stove oven. While that was baking I chopped up several stalks of fresh rhubarb, added some sugar, and simmered it until the sugar melted and the rhubarb was tender and juicy. I had started a pot of pinto beans simmering this morning, adding some chopped ham. Dan moaned that the kitchen smells were driving him crazy. We ate early, topping off supper with the cake and rhubarb sauce. Dan insisted on cleaning up the kitchen while I bathed in the banya. He is washing up now, and when he returns he'll tell me more about the ancient people of Kodiak Island. I hope the weather is nice tomorrow, since I am very anxious to work at the barabara again. Just a few months ago a very different Marie lived in Seattle.

July 10—We were out in the rain this morning, and I took a bad fall, bruising my hip. Something more serious than the injury happened. Dan helped me get my legs back under me on the slippery grass, and his hand held onto mine longer than necessary, I think. I am attracted to this quiet man in a way I never thought possible, but he is married—and come to think of it, so am I. Since the rain kept us from working at the site this afternoon, we spent the time cleaning the cabin, and later I read awhile. I avoided looking straight at Dan, and I believe he was doing the same. After dinner I said I was very tired, and crawled into my bunk to read a little more. Dan had his small lantern burning on the table, working on his field notes. I was worried that he might think I am angry at him, so I broke his concentration over the table by asking if he thought we would be rained out again tomorrow. He pushed back from the table, seemingly relieved I had asked, and said "Sure feels like it!" Then he said he would stir up a batch of sourdough "sponge" to sit overnight, so we could bake some bread tomorrow. I'm going to try not to think of how his hand felt, closing over mine.

July 11—Dan was right about the rain; it kept up all night and pounded hard on the roof all day. We were snug as a bug in the little cabin, heated up when we baked our 2 loaves of sourdough bread. Dan showed me how he removes a half cup of the sponge which contains the yeast, each time before using the rest for baking. The half cup is stored in a cool cabinet and will be used to start the next batch of sponge. He showed me how to mix in more flour, salt, sugar, and melted lard; then I stirred and kneaded it. After the ball of dough had risen in a greased bowl, which takes 2 or 3 hours, I shaped it into two loaves to rise again. Dan desperately needed a hair trim, so I took care of that job. We worked on sketches until the bread was baked. I made hot beef and gravy with some canned roast, and ladled it over thick slices of warm bread. Dan declared it was just like his mother used to make. The wind started blowing during the evening, but the rain seems to have moved on.

July 12—Today we awoke to a beautiful sight, which was the sun! Dan suggested we take a hike east of the cabin, instead of going straight to the dig. We began by walking along the beach, and I noticed tiny hoof prints dotting our path. Following the deer tracks up a narrow trail through the willows, we topped a knob which provided a great view of a broad valley. In the distance I could just make out a looping river entering a thick forest. Dan said it was the same river where Ivan and I were camped. He said its name is Little Bear River; however I told him I was re-christening it *Ivan's River*. A herd of deer meandered across the valley, nibbling on the willows. Dan says deer were not native to Kodiak, but Sitka Black Tail deer were introduced in the

1920's, and are now found across much of the island. After we crossed several small streams, we watched a family of river otters sliding along the rocks and tumbling with each other, like a group of school kids. The adults are about three feet long, dark brown and sleek. Dan told me they like nothing better than to crawl into an anchored boat, and take turns diving off the sides. I have found that I am falling in love with this wilderness, wanting to learn more and more about my surroundings. We got back to the cabin about lunch time, and after eating some more of that good bread, we headed for the dig. I wanted to sketch into this journal a pair of eagles that have been lurking around the beach near the dig. Hiding behind some alders a little distance from the beach, I sketched for about two hours. Checking to see what Dan was doing, I saw him kneeling in the trench, taking photos; his brown hair had fallen over his forehead, and smudges of soot from a fire pit he uncovered were along his jaw where he must have brushed away a mosquito or gnat. I had to admire his concentration. Suddenly he looked up in my direction, and caught me staring right at him. I was very embarrassed but when he focused the camera on me, I exaggerated a silly pose and we laughed. He waved me down to the site to show off a slate knife he had just uncovered. We took more photos of each other showing off the knife and parts of the site. I actually think he likes having someone with whom to share his treasures. Me! Tonight Dan insisted on cleaning up the dinner dishes while I visited the banya. Tomorrow we are going to check out an interesting outcrop of rock beyond the barabara.

July 13—My adventure here gets more confusing every day. Today we made our way to the rock face, being buffeted by the wind gusting down the lake. The outcrop that rises about ten feet above the bear trail, appeared to taper back into the knoll of the western ridge above the lake. Suddenly, Dan grabbed my shoulders, shoved me up against the rock, and leaned tightly against my whole body. I was shocked and did not understand until he murmured into my ear to stay very still, as a bear was crossing closely upwind of us. My face was pressed into his flannel shirt at the shoulder. My heart was pounding, but soon I realized it wasn't because of the bear danger. Dan relaxed after a few minutes, but his arms still held me tight. With a slight tremble, his hand stroked my hair. My knees threatened to give way, never had I felt such tenderness. I could tell he was breathing in my scent, and I was intoxicated with his closeness. Finally he awkwardly stepped back, and checked the area to be safe. He pointed down the beach, and we could see the rump of a huge brownie slowly making his way, oblivious of our presence, thank goodness. It started to rain again, so we left our exploration to another day, and returned to the cabin where Dan worked on his notes, and I finished up my sketch of the eagles. We spoke only in general terms about our day, marveling at our close encounter. He was talking about the bear, and I was thinking about him.

July 14—Today Dan uncovered a rock slab in the floor of the barabara. He explained that sometimes such rocks cover a storage hole, much like our cooler box under the cabin's wooden floor. He was right! When the slab was moved, we found several small tools in the shallow niche. Some were made from bone and others were slate, but most looked like chisels in various sizes. What looked like a fist-sized rock at first, Dan said was actually a tool used to tap the chisels, to mark or decorate something. This evening Dan asked more about my life before Kodiak. We were busy working on the sketches of the day, and I was taken by surprise at his question. I told him about my family and how my parents had died. I also told him how I met Ed, and I even read a few journal entries from the spring. He was so genuinely saddened. I began crying and couldn't talk anymore. He said he was so sorry he brought it up, but I told him it actually helped to have someone to tell. I admitted that although I don't want to go back to my husband, I am afraid of what would happen if Ed ever caught up with me. Remaining dead for now is fine, but how hard would it be to stay that way? Dan laughed, as if to put aside all the serious talk, and exclaimed "you don't look very dead." Funny, in my whole life I have never felt so alive.

July 15—This morning was sunny and warm, so we decided to hike up to the ridge. I asked Dan how far I would have had to follow the river from where Ivan and I were stranded before getting help. He pointed to a far off horizon and estimated it would have taken a man who knew the terrain, at least two days to reach the coast going that way. Bear encounters would have likely been frequent, but if I had known not to panic and run, it might have ended alright. When the bears have a plentiful salmon supply, they don't usually care about humans, unless you get too close and threatening. There was always a chance I might have come across some hunters or fishermen on the river, but most likely not. Dan assured me that I did all I could for Ivan, and I shouldn't feel guilty for not striking out for help. As we were hiking back down to the cabin two small deer ran across our path, the first I had seen up close. Dan says they roam mostly in the meadows, and along the beaches. After working at the site this afternoon, Dan bent over the table, engrossed in his field notes, while I made a tuna casserole. I noticed he had a copy of *Last of the Mohicans* on the bookshelf, and when I began reading it in my bunk this evening, Dan asked if I liked to read aloud. We have decided I'll read at least one chapter every night.

July 16—Dan told me more about the hunting camp he had mentioned walking to for help, when Ivan and I arrived. He wants me to know where it is in case of an emergency, and I teased, like when a bear eats him? He got the map and showed me how to make my way to the distant bay, including a lesson in reading a compass. Ironically, with our heads bent over the maps, I felt sort of a magnetic pull towards him, and had to concentrate on not swaying in his direction. A bead of moisture broke out across my upper lip, and I felt a tightening in my chest and couldn't breathe evenly. I am almost certain he noticed, but finally I made an excuse that I needed to pack up a lunch for us. We spent most of the day working at the site, brushing grains of earth from tiny knobs protruding from the side of the trench. Perhaps we will uncover another surprise, like the lamp. Dan told me that it was common to find tiny "hunter's lamps" in temporary camps, but not one this size. Research has revealed the native people came inland during the summer, and with the warm temperatures and light, why would they need a large lamp? The markings decorating it were more evident once we brushed the dirt from all the grooves. Dan says these designs are sometimes colored, and made fast with blood. This evening after he made his notes, Dan brought out his violin and played while I worked on a sketch of our cabin and Lost Lake. I do love getting to work with the pencils and paper again. Ed had no right to deny me that joy. If I ever see Ed again, he will be shocked at the changes in his wife. I am trim, and feel younger than I have since college.

July 17—Today we found two more ancient tools to add to the box of similar items. These are pointed bone implements that Dan explains would be used for gouging and etching other tools or house wares. The mystery is that we haven't found anything that was decorated except the stone lamp. Why would they have such tools here? The site is not consistent with other excavations. What compelled the people to return to this place over so many years? Was it like a pilgrimage? Dan admits he is obsessed with solving this mystery, and I'll admit I am very curious. When I began sketching the implements this evening, Dan interrupted, insisting that it was time I had a shooting lesson! What will he think of next? There was plenty of daylight left, so I agreed and followed him outside. He showed me how to load the rifle, and set up some targets. It's not really so important to hit a bulls-eye, since he hoped it would only be used to scare curious bears away. The stock of this rifle (an old 30/06 Springfield) is too long for my arms, so I can't snug it up into my shoulder quite enough. If I am careful and not in too much of a hurry, I can manage to get it firmly planted so it doesn't kick too much.

July 18—I found a deposit of pulverized red ochre in a large clam shell buried at the site. This prize was nestled in the back end of the barabara. This means that the ancient people were indeed using their time here decorating things, but what? Dan suggested that we take the rest of the day off since he wanted to do some reading on Hrdlicka's excavations, and also some of what Frederica de Laguna found in Kachemak Bay in the 1930's. Before leaving the site, he asked if I would pose for a photo, showing off the ochre shell. I spent the afternoon cleaning the little cabin, and baking bread. While the bread was rising, I took time to wash my hair and bathe in the banya. The clothes I have are too large now; even Ivan's blue jeans are loose, but I feel strong and healthy. We had a dinner of beef stew made from some canned meat and the last of our fresh vegetables, plus slices of fresh bread. Dan shared with me some of what he read on earlier discoveries, and I find it fascinating. Later I read aloud, since Dan seemed to want to stretch the evening out. Before turning out his lantern, he talked of his excitement over the pointed tools and red ochre. I will turn out my light, but I don't think I'll be able to sleep.

July 19—Dan worked at the site a couple of hours this morning, and I stretched out on sweet smelling hillside grass to sketch some tiny yellow and pink flowers pushing their way out of a rock crevice. We were forced to give up when it began to rain, and by the time we made it to the cabin the wind had picked up. I made a rhubarb pie, and worked on sketches while it baked. When it had cooled enough to cut, Dan declared it was the best pie ever!

July 20—Dan shot a deer today. He came across an injured one while exploring some low hills north of the dig. He was actually looking for some ripe salmonberries, when he saw the deer laying in a gully. It had apparently fallen and broken its back, so Dan put it out of its misery. He quickly dressed and packed most of it back to the cabin. It seems that the weather is too warm to let the meat hang, so we will butcher it tomorrow. Since we are out of fresh meat in the cooler box, this will be a welcome addition to our menus. We ended the evening as usual, with more chapters from the book.

July 21—It didn't take any time at all for Dan to cut up the meat, since these deer are much smaller than their cousins down south. When he trimmed off some steaks, I fried some for our lunch. What a treat! I simmered some chunks and put them in lidded jars. Weighted down with rocks in the cold stream, the meat will stay good for a few days. Since we don't have any other good way to preserve the remainder of the meat, Dan says he'll make jerky. Saving back a nice roast, he sliced thin strips of the remaining meat, salted and peppered in preparation for the smokehouse. After the strips have hung overnight on the wires crisscrossing the shed, Dan will build a small, smoldering fire, using dry alder. After about two days, Dan says the end product will be preserved and ready to eat.

July 22—I can see a wisp of smoke escaping from our improvised smokehouse. Dan spent most of the day at the dig while I baked bread and slow-cooked the deer roast. Since it was a sunny day, I washed a few small things. This evening we both are very tired and by the time I had cleaned up, Dan was dozing over his papers. He just roused and said he'd smoke a pipe full and check on the smokehouse.

July 23—Last night Dan came back into the cabin, turned out the lantern and crawled into his bunk. In the darkness he said, "Marie" and I said "Yes?" Then he said "I have to tell you that these weeks have been…uh…a nice surprise." And I replied, "For me too". We were silent for a moment, then he just said "Goodnight" and I said "'Night." But it was a long time before I fell asleep. This morning I tidied up Ivan's grave and transplanted some wild flowers to a spot near the marker. Dan says wildflowers don't transplant well, and they will most likely die. Before leaving for the site, Dan said that the supply plane would be showing up sometime in the next week. He has written a couple of letters for the pilot to mail for him, and left them on the table for pickup, in case he isn't at the cabin when the plane comes. I won't snoop to see who they are for. I am still trying to decide what to do when that plane shows up. Should I return to Seattle, and shock Ed with my story of survival? Would I be able to tell him I spent weeks alone with another man and no longer want to be his wife? Or would he still be able to intimidate me into being afraid to leave? We both worked quietly at the dig this afternoon. Dan seemed lost in thought and I tried to concentrate only on the work in my hands.

By 4:00 we headed back to the cabin. Dan checked the smokehouse contents and declared the jerky is perfect. We ate leftovers for supper and jerky for dessert! Dan played his violin for about an hour, and then I read the end of *Last of the Mohicans.*

July 24—This evening Dan managed to put a small but nasty gash in his forehead near the hairline. He said he forgot to duck when rounding the low eave of the banya, returning from the hillside with a pail full of salmonberries. Dan let me clean the cut, but it turned into an awkward moment for us both. He sat on the edge of his bunk, which put his head about even with mine. Suddenly I couldn't keep my hands from shaking. Dan asked if I was going to faint, and he put his hands on my waist. His touch was electric. Our eyes met for a moment. Oh my god, I know he could see that I wanted him to kiss me right then. I broke eye contact, realizing I had to stop this fantasy, and pulled away. Fumbling with the first aid box, I declared I had done all I could do. Dan mumbled he needed to check something outside. When he returned, I was busy sketching another clamshell of ochre that Dan unearthed today. Later I read aloud from a collection of short stories by Jack London, which prevented us from having to do any small talk.

July 25—I spent a sleepless night, but have decided to catch the plane when it shows up. It isn't fair to Dan for me to stay. I know I am in love with him, but how could I not be? He is all I ever wanted. I told Dan that I would put a note by his letters, telling the pilot to wait for a passenger, in case we are not at the cabin. He seemed surprised, and started to say something, but reconsidered and turned away. Today was foggy so we knew the plane would not arrive. We did manage to have a good time at the dig, although both of us were rather somber. Dan found another bone tool that appears to have been useful for prying or scraping. Tonight I completed the sketch, and when I handed it to him, he laid it aside and asked me if returning to Ed was my true wish. I couldn't answer him for a minute, but managed to stammer that it was best. I quickly added that I had some ideas for handling the situation at home. In truth, I had no idea what I was going to do. Dan looked hard at me, holding my gaze, and asked if I were afraid to stay here, alone with him any longer. Tears in my eyes welled up and I turned away as if to straighten my blankets on the bunk. I shook my head and did not remind him that each of us belong to another. We each lay in our bunks, listening to the storm brewing, feeling the cabin shudder against each gust.

July 26—Dan has made, in his own words, "the discovery of a lifetime!" Last night the wind tore off a piece of the banya's roof, so Dan went to the site for a tarp we use on drizzly days. The tarp had blown away from the site, and lodged against the edge of the rock face we were going to explore awhile back. He noticed that part of the face was not solid rock at all, but animal bones and smaller stacked rocks. Dan carefully started pulling them away when he realized that they were covering an opening. He was running back to our cabin, when I met him on the trail, and we quickly gathered some tools and a lantern. After an hour's work, taking photographs as we removed the barrier, we managed to slip thru the opening into a narrow cave. It tapered back for about fifteen feet, becoming much smaller as it went. We scanned the floor with our lantern, looking for signs of human or animal habitation, but none were apparent. As we turned back toward the narrow entrance slit, the lantern's glow reflected on the cave's ceiling, and we both gasped! Engraved into the stone ceiling and upper walls were dozens of figures, easily seen to be human and animal forms. It appeared the scenes had been painstakingly etched, the grooves colored with some material, perhaps soot and the red ochre. We both were speechless and sat in the cave for a long time, taking in the scenes. We now know why the stone lamp was needed. How many years have passed since a human figure sat on this cave floor admiring the drawings? What an honor it will be to copy them. Dan has used all of his flash bulb supply, so we must make drawings to show the placement of the figures, as well as detailed sketches. We returned to the cabin to make sandwiches, and gather our sketching materials and the other lantern. All the while, I was hoping that the plane would not arrive today. I took a photo of Dan outside the cave, pointing out the opening. We worked late, mostly examining each figure in detail, making just a few sketches. Finally our stomachs insisted dinner was overdue! I am so excited to work on this discovery!

July 27—Thank goodness today is very overcast and foggy, so I get at least one more day here. Dan explained how rare these petroglyphs are, with only one other similar site having been discovered on Kodiak Island so far. Hrdlicka wrote that some at Cape Alitak found in the open, were attributed to pre-Koniag people. Dan has a theory that our Lost Lake cave drawings might have been designated a magical or religious location by the pre-Koniags. Perhaps they produced the drawings to celebrate their prowess as hunters, returning occasionally to get empowered in the spirit of future hunts. Somehow the oral history of this cave was forgotten, since there is no evidence this site has been visited in hundreds of years. Many of the drawings depict human figures, some with spears or drums. Dan says the style of art is very similar to what was found at Cape Alitak. We can identify the animals, although they are what I would call stylized. An elongated body with eyes and antlers must represent caribou. Even the pre-Koniag people were known to venture to the mainland across Shelikof Strait in their little skin boats to hunt the herds of caribou. Some of the etchings are of human heads, with large eyes in very round faces. I don't know what the Y shaped figures mean, but they are abundant. We could identify whales, seals, foxes, fish and birds. Dan and I worked feverishly on mapping out a grid to organize our sketches of the ceiling. Finally my neck muscles rebelled and Dan admitted he had to call it a day. We are two exhausted, happy people this evening.

July 28—The morning was blustery and wet, but we went to the cave anyway. After working a few hours, we had to give up, since the cave was so cold that our fingers couldn't stay warm enough to make decent sketches! I washed my hair and later made a pan of cornbread. I used some of the cooked venison to make a thick stew. In the evening, Dan read aloud from Hrdlicka's *Anthropology of Kodiak Island*. This discovery will someday be part of a new publication, written by Dan!

July 29—This morning we awoke to a clear, blue sky, perfect for flying. I had a lump in my throat because I felt that this day the plane would come. We breakfasted on the last of our bacon, with toast and gravy. I decided to go to the cave for awhile, so we struck out with a loaf of bread, a hunk of cheese and a thermos of coffee (what, no wine?). We worked quickly, somehow feeling that we had to make up for the work missed yesterday. I found that the best position for viewing the petroglyphs is to lay on my back on a wool blanket, with my head propped up on the small backpack. Once we get the grids sketched with the basic layout of designs, I will begin reproducing each grid square in detail. Dan also is working on the grid layout, but will leave the details to me. We don't speak aloud about my leaving soon, not being part of the finished product. Dan is always complimentary of my work, and I never felt so important before this. On our return to the cabin this evening, I found myself wondering if I would be able to leave Dan this week. I wanted him to tell me that everything will be O.K., no matter what. All afternoon I kept expecting to hear the sound of a plane approaching. When the sun finally set, I felt lucky to have had one more day with Dan.

July 30—Today is Dan's birthday, so I gave him the sketch I made of our little cabin by the lake. He declared it would have a prominent place in his office. My heart hurts when I think of what I missed all these years. When Dan is out of my sight, I wait impatiently for his head to pop up over the hill; at the sound of his footstep at the door, I feel a catch in my throat that gives way to a secret smile. Even though I cannot have him, I don't regret this time together. I have learned that kindness and affection are the feelings I crave in a man. I will not settle for less again. Still, no plane!

July 31—We hardly take time to rest in our haste to get the sketches and notes finished. According to Dan, this site is what the people in his field dream about. He will just gather all the data and the winter will be spent analyzing and putting it into a presentable format. We spotted one of the big brownies this afternoon, meandering along the lake's shoreline near the original barabara. When he saw us, he bolted over the bluff into an alder thicket. I wish we could have seen him scamper on over the far ridge, so I would know he was really out of our territory. Right now I feel like he is just waiting for us to leave so he can come right back to the shore. This evening Dan fished for awhile and brought me a beautiful salmon to cut into steaks. We laughed about our Five-Star restaurant menu, and again I watched the sun set with no plane in sight. Just before we went to our respective bunks, Dan handed me a folded sliver of paper. When I saw that he had written his phone number in Fairbanks on it, he quietly asked me to call him if I ever needed help.

August 1—I am waiting for Dan to join me at the cabin. He should be here soon, but so much happened today that I can't describe in words how I feel right this minute! I suppose I could say I am walking on air, but very confused. This morning I decided to stay at the cabin while Dan worked at the cave. We talked about the drawings as he gathered supplies. His plan was to work in the cave a few hours, but he instructed me that if the plane comes I should have the pilot wait until he can reach the cabin, for a final good-bye. Dan took my hand, and said he had known only one other woman who was so brave. He asked if he could help me in any way and I said it would only be worse if he got involved. I assured him I would get a good lawyer, and stay away from Ed. My heart was wrenched as I remembered the fine days and evenings we had shared. I truly believe that I may never care for a man as I have come to care for Dan. It's hard to let him think I don't notice his eyes on me as we work at the table, or the lingering touches. After watching Ed's attentions for another woman, I never wanted to inflict that pain on another man's wife. Watching as he walked down the trail towards the cave, I felt as if I would never be the same when he is not part of my life. The day dragged out, and by mid-afternoon I convinced myself the plane was not going to come to Lost Lake today. Suddenly the drone of an approaching aircraft announced the sight of a plane dipping onto the other end of the lake. Before I could think twice, I grabbed my note for the pilot, stepped around back of the cabin, and skirted some brush before hiding behind the banya. After securing the float plane in the shallows, the pilot carried several boxes of supplies into the cabin. Twice he yelled for Dan, but gave up and I noticed he returned to the plane with the letters that had been left on the table. Was I right in staying? One second I was ready to run to the plane, but I just couldn't make myself take the first step. I caught a movement to my left and a chill went through me that a bear had caught me being careless. I turned, dreading what I would see, but about 100 feet away, in a willow patch, stood Dan looking straight at me. He made no movement to alert the pilot and neither did I. Finally the plane took off in a storm of spray and noise. When it banked over the hills, Dan stepped away from the willows and walked toward me without taking his eyes off mine. I stumbled from my hiding place towards him. We met, and stood apart for a moment. I answered his questioning look by blurting "I missed the plane!" He smiled and stepped closer. I knew what I felt, but what was Dan doing? He asked, "Are you still avoiding Ed, or did you stay for another reason?" I could only manage to say, "It's you." He took my shoulders in his big hands. Dan then moved his hands up on each side of my face before leaning down to plant the sweetest kiss on my surprised mouth. I started to step back but he enveloped me tightly in his strong arms, kissing me gently and hard at the same time. When we stepped apart both of us were tearful, and I pulled him to me again as I could not get enough of the feel of him against me. He murmured in my hair, "You are not facing Ed alone." With my arm around his waist and his around my shoulders, we slowly walked back to the cabin, stopping two or three times for another heavenly kiss. The rest of the afternoon made me forget all my concerns. I can't describe the feelings I have for this man. If this summer is all I get of him, I will be happy for the rest of my life. He has gone to collect the lantern from the cave while I fix something to eat. He says he has something to explain to me this evening.

August 2—Dan is badly hurt. After he didn't return last evening, I searched and found where he had fallen on slick rocks while skirting the lake on his way back from the cave. His right leg below the knee has a terrible break, the bone almost puncturing the skin. He is in such pain, but I managed to splint his leg and drag him to the cabin. We have to get some help. The hunting lodge is his only chance. I must get there and radio for help. I am making these notes and leaving my journal with Dan. If I become lost, or somehow do not reach help, someone will eventually show up and the story of our situation will be known. Dan is against my going, saying I don't have a good chance of finding the lodge, and could die before finding anyone. He says that if I stay here, I will at least be ok until the plane comes back. But I will not stay and watch him die like Ivan. I have the map that Dan showed me. Following the beach past the cave to the other end of the lake, I'll reach the small river flowing out of the lake, and I am to follow it through the low hills and brush. After about a day following the river, I will notice it bends sharply to the northwest just after passing a large bluff. At that point I turn east. Dan estimates that it will take me almost two more days to reach the bay where the lodge is. The hardest part, he says, will be right after leaving the river, where the only trails are made by bears through head-high berry bushes, alder and devil's club growth. Dan says the last part should be mostly rolling, grassy slopes to the bay. I have packed the compass, map, machete', a canteen, some jerky and bread, matches, blanket and rain gear. Dan insists that I carry the rifle in case I have to scare off a bear. Since I will keep the rifle loaded, I have to make sure the safety is on except when I plan to use it. He warns me to make a lot of noise, singing, yelling, anything to warn the bears I am coming. I shouldn't try to sneak through their territory, unless I see one far away and am downwind of him. I am placing some containers of water and food near Dan, but I doubt he will eat much. I took time this morning to fashion an SOS on the beach with fuel cans and rocks. If, on the outside chance, someone were to fly over in the next few days, at least Dan would be saved. He is feverish and in much pain. I wish we had something to help. He keeps saying he has to tell me something, but I have to leave.

Rosalie laid the journal on her lap and said quietly, "That's the end of it." Penny exclaimed, "You are kidding!"

Rosalie thumbed back through the pages, and remarked, "This woman loved that man so much, and obviously he feels something for her, but I just don't understand. I hope they both lived to sort it out."

Penny agreed, "What a love story. I can't stand not knowing what happened!"

"Hey, maybe we can research online about the archaeological finds on Kodiak Island, and get some more information about Dan," Penny added.

Rosalie unwound herself from the blanket and stretched, tempted to spend the night on Penny's sofa. Remembering how hectic her daughter's mornings are, Rosalie opted for a quiet breakfast with Ray, so that was worth the 15 minute drive home.

Later, as she crept down the hall to the bathroom, her husband called out from the bedroom, "So did you girls have a good time?"

"I can't believe you're awake. I'll be there in a minute."

Finally, in her pajamas, and droopy eyed, Rosalie curled up to Ray's back. For some reason she felt compelled to tell him she loved him, but he was already asleep.

Over a waffle breakfast, Rosalie shared with Ray what she and Penny read, and he agreed that they should track down the diary's owner. Surely a family would not have meant to dispose of it. Ray called the auction company, and when told of the personal journal, they offered to call the consignor. If the previous owner wanted the item back, Ray's phone number would be given.

The next evening Rosalie answered the phone, and the unmistakable voice of an elderly woman identified herself as the Marie who penned the journal. Rosalie couldn't believe her luck, actually talking to the real Marie! She couldn't wait to tell Penny that Marie survived.

"I had so many people helping me box up my houseful of things, I think some boxes were given to the auction house, instead of being delivered to my new apartment," Marie explained.

Rosalie told her how happy she was to get the journal into the right hands. "I could mail it to you, but I would be happy to deliver it personally." Of course she was anxious to meet this remarkable woman.

"Oh, I am so thankful that you took the trouble to find me. I would love to meet you," Marie said. She was not at all surprised when Rosalie admitted that she and her daughter Penny had read the journal. Marie justified it for Rosalie, "After all, if you hadn't, you might not have felt the need to find me! Bring your daughter, too!"

Recently widowed, Marie had just moved into a senior apartment complex in Gresham, Oregon, just a few miles from Rosalie's book shop. After checking with Penny, they decided to arrive at Marie's apartment the next Sunday afternoon when Driftwood Books was closed, and Penny's husband could take care of the boys. At last Sunday arrived, with Rosalie and Penny as giddy as teenagers. Marie had been watching for them, and opened the front door before Rosalie had a chance to knock. Apologizing for the cluttered living room and hall, she explained that her son would be coming later to help her hang pictures, and put storage boxes in the top of her closets.

Marie was a little taller than Rosalie had envisioned, and not as frail as her voice sounded. Her eyes were as violet as the irises in Rosalie's flower garden. Short silvery hair and a delicate purple scarf tied loosely around her neck framed her face. Marie moved fluidly, belying the fact she must be about eighty-six. Later, Penny and Rosalie discussed how warm Marie's smile was, putting them at ease when discussing the personal parts of her life.

Marie suggested they take the prepared iced tea to the stone patio off the kitchen; it was surrounded by flowering shrubs, and furnished with comfortable outdoor furniture. Rosalie took the journal from her purse, and presented it to Marie, saying "I think this belongs to you."

"I can't believe I let this slip away. You don't know how much this means to me," Marie confided to the two women.

Penny said, "You have such a gift of describing your experiences. As we read your entries, I felt like we were right there with you." Rosalie nodded in agreement.

"As you know, the journal was given to me by my sister. I found that writing down thoughts about my life with Ed helped me realize I had to get away from him. When Ivan and I were alone by the river, writing in the journal helped me get through every day, one day at a time." As she spoke, Marie clutched the small book to her breast.

Rosalie said, "Penny and I were so happy to find out that you survived, after reading of those weeks at Lost Lake. Please tell us about Dan."

Marie leaned back in her chair and propped her feet upon a low ottoman. She almost chuckled, saying, "I'll start where the journal ended, and my real adventure began." Rosalie refrained from the impulse to clap her hands; instead she settled back in her lounge chair.

"The trail around the lake as far as the cave was so familiar I could almost believe that Dan was right behind me. Upon reaching the cave, I ducked my head inside but it was too dark to see the figures on the ceiling. I used the moment to psyche myself up, thinking of the hunters inscribed by the ancient artists. After all, they only had spears and rocks and I had the rifle and a map.

"As I followed the edge of the lake, bear sign was everywhere; droppings and fish carcasses were strewn and rotting along the way. It's funny how those big bears are so picky when fish are plentiful. They just take a big chunk from the belly area where most of the fat is, and leave the rest. I remember thinking that since they are so full of fish, they would not be interested in a skinny woman. After being away from the cabin for over an hour, I came to the small river that I had to follow. I turned to look back up the lake towards the cabin, hoping I could see it one more time, but it just wasn't possible. The riverbank was slick, paved with algae-covered rocks. Dan said it would be best to walk along the river where I had a better view of my path, instead of up on the low grassy bluff that might hide a dozing bear. Occasionally I would spot a salmon's back as it thrashed in the shallows trying to make headway upstream. It reminded me of Ivan catching one for our dinner so long ago. I had the rifle ready, and all of a sudden I had a reason to use it. About one hundred feet from me, near a bend in the river, a large bear was concentrating on catching a fish for his dinner. He hadn't seen me yet, but he must have caught my scent because he reared up and put his snout in the air. When he started swinging his massive head back and forth, I brought the rifle to my shoulder and pulled the trigger. Nothing happened! Panic almost froze my brain, but then I realized I had forgotten to push the safety off. With the click of that safety, my confidence returned. I fired off a round into the air, which did just what it is supposed to do; the bear fell back to all fours and disappeared over the bank, into the brush."

Marie took a sip of tea, and Rosalie asked, "Weren't you petrified? I would have fainted!"

Laughing, Marie replied, "I didn't have time for that. The recoil of the rifle had knocked me down, and I was frantically trying to stand up in case I needed to shoot again. Oh, my shoulder hurt from that one shot, and later I found a huge black bruise there. I then remembered that I might possibly have avoided the bear encounter, if I had been singing and making other warning noises as I walked. That bear most likely would have already been alerted to my approach, and been on his way. I didn't forget that again.

"Since I had been successful at avoiding bears on the trails around our camp, I used the tactics Ivan taught me. I stopped walking well before dark, since the most dangerous times for surprising a bear are at evening dusk and early daylight. I picked out a spot along the river where I had a large boulder at my back, and I built two large fires in front of where I stretched out. To prepare for the long night, I stacked up a good supply of anything I could find that would burn, mostly alder downfall. I wasn't hungry but knew it was important to eat so I managed to choke down a slice of bread, some jerky, a Baby Ruth, and water.

"Going against what Dan had instructed, the safety on the rifle by my side was left ready to fire. Sleep didn't really come, but I lightly dozed. The fires had to be replenished every hour or so; thank goodness it wasn't raining. When I first wrapped up in the blanket and leaned back against the boulder, I was so terrified my teeth chattered. I think I was on the verge of going into shock. I started talking to myself about how well the afternoon had gone, and along with getting my body very warm by the campfire, I managed to calm down.

Rosalie noticed that Marie's expression had become sad, and a glint of tears shown in her eyes. Neither Rosalie nor Penny made a remark as they waited for her to continue.

"Dan was in my thoughts most of the night, of course. His injury was so bad I worried he would die of an infection or shock before help could arrive. Being alone, I was scared and overwhelmed with the rescue try. Later I could see the stars, and remembered the evenings Dan and I spent watching them appear as the darkness descended at the late hour in Alaska. It was strange to think that these were the same stars we saw on clear nights, after a wonderful day at the dig, or after he serenaded me with his sweet music; those memories kept me sane the first night. During the night, little animals skittered all around scratching at tree bark, rustling the leaves. A deer family watched as I built the fires up sometime after midnight; their four pairs of eyes reflected the firelight, giving away their positions in the darkness."

Since the tension had lessened in Marie's voice, Penny asked, "Did you hear or see any bears that night?"

"No, thank goodness!" Marie exclaimed. "I might not have been able to go on if I had."

"Oh, I think you would have," Rosalie said, and Marie smiled at her insight.

"I woke with the daylight, and found that a thick fog lay over the land that muffled even the sounds of the river. I waited an hour for the fog to lift, ate a little and decided to set out. I headed down river, singing *Oh My Darling, Clementine* at the top of my lungs! The slick rocks along the bank caused me so much grief, and I fell several times. I was so afraid I would break a leg and be stranded, with no rescue for either of us. Another concern I had was missing the big bend in the river that would signal where I would leave the river and head over the hills. I consulted the compass often, and as luck would have it, the fog lifted by noon. About 2:00 I recognized the bluff from what Dan had described and just beyond was the sharp western bend in the river. As I turned away from the river, the compass indeed indicated my direction was eastward. I tried to pick a spot to enter the tangle of Devil's Club branches, using the machete to whack some out of my way. Those plants are over head-high, and the stalks are covered with thousands of spines. Even the leaves are mean! The stalks are about an inch in diameter, and springy, so if you whack one at the wrong spot or angle, it bounces back and hits you."

Rosalie interrupted, "How well I know that! Ray and I were camping in British Columbia a few years ago. I took a short cut back to the camper one afternoon, and ended up in a green hell!"

Everyone laughed, agreeing that the Devil's Club moniker fit perfectly.

Penny refilled the tea glasses while Marie sliced fresh banana bread. Rosalie asked to use Marie's bathroom; on the way back to the patio, she noticed a framed print leaning against the leg of an end table. When Rosalie bent for a closer look, it took only a minute for her to identify the oval image sketched in pencil. The shallow bowl had a whale's tail decorating the bottom. Rosalie jerked upright, exclaiming, "The stone lamp!"

Marie overheard the remark, "Yes, the stone lamp. That sketch has always been my favorite of all the drawings that summer. I gave the real lamp to the museum in Kodiak."

The three women settled into their patio chairs once more. Marie continued, pausing occasionally to nibble on the banana bread.

"After struggling through the brush for about two hours, I stumbled onto a trail, obviously made by bears, but I used it! Switching to *She Wore a Yellow Ribbon*, I sang until I was hoarse. To stay heading east I had to leave the bear trail. It seemed that when I walked out of a patch of devil's club, I would run into a patch of alder, growing so thickly intertwined it was difficult to drag myself under, over, and through the mess. Most branches were too thick to be cut by the machete, so very often I had to dodge off course. The rifle was becoming very heavy, and hard to manage through the tangle, but I wouldn't think of putting it down. The alders were so thick in some places that I couldn't see much beyond 10 feet. I sang very loud, and twice that afternoon I heard big animals crash away from my path. I can only guess what they were.

"There were times throughout the day when I visualized Dan, laying on his bunk, in pain and sick with worry about me. I had to keep telling myself that everything would be alright, once I got to the lodge. It all depended on me unless some pilot saw my SOS on the beach.

"My feet were beginning to be a problem. I had decided to wear Ivan's boots, but they were proving too sloppy for walking long distances. My feet had become wet the first day out, and I was afraid to remove my boots that night, which was a mistake. On this second evening I picked a place to camp about 8:00. My campsite was beside a tiny stream, barely a foot wide, but at least I could fill my canteen. In the back of my mind I knew the risk of getting ill from some germ in the untreated water, just as Ivan said. I built up a large campfire again, and decided to peel off my boots and socks. Oh, my feet were raw in many places, but it felt good to prop them up alongside the fire, being careful to not get blistered. Thankfully, I had packed the tennis shoes that were my main footwear for the summer. Those, with a pair of dry socks, were better than the boots. I hadn't seen any bear sign the last two hours of my walk, so I wasn't so scared that night.

"Chewing on a piece of jerky made me remember the day we butchered the deer. I also thought of how I felt when Dan pulled me close and kissed me for the first time. This led to thinking about our afternoon together and Dan's tenderness. Holding onto those good thoughts, I threw another couple of branches on the fire and wrapped up in the blanket. Fatigue rescued me from worry, as sleep came quickly and deeply. About 2:00 in the morning I woke to build up the fire, afterwards dozing off and on. With daylight came wind and rain, so I pulled out Dan's rain jacket and gave up on the idea of dry feet.

"From Dan's map I estimated I was halfway to the lodge, if I hadn't veered off too much north or south in dodging outcrops, tangled alders and devil's club. Had I known how difficult this day would be, I might have turned back for the cabin. It poured rain all morning, so every little knoll, rock, grassy slope, piece of alder I had to climb over…everything was slick. Sometimes when I'd crest a hill, the wind would almost blow me off my feet. I was so tempted to curl up inside a shelter of alder branches, but couldn't afford to lose the time. The day almost came undone when I took a bad spill down a slick embankment into a ravine about 12 feet deep. Dazed for a bit, I managed to collect my wits, and examined the rifle for damage. The old beat up stock was more scarred than ever, but it seemed to be ok. When I tried to climb back up the slope, I would just slide back down after a few feet. That plan was hopeless, so I decided to follow the ravine and find a better place to climb out. Spending at least an hour searching, I finally came to a place where the ravine was not as steep, and some rocky ledges provided footholds. Reaching the top, I realized that I must be awfully off course. I followed the ravine rim back to about where I fell in, so I could set my eastward course again. Suddenly I found that my stamina had given out, and I was shaking all over from exhaustion. Wet and cold, muddy from head to foot, I slumped to the ground under an old growth of thick elderberry bushes. I broke down crying, sobbing actually. Finally I made myself breathe deeply through my nose to keep from hyperventilating. I felt so lonely and scared, even kind of mad.

Rosalie asked, "Was there any hope you would run into people out there…like hunters?"

"Dan didn't think so. He didn't know of any guide who used that area for clients, and the native villages were way up the coast."

"Miraculously, the rain started to let up, so I rooted under the brush to find some dry twigs. After getting the little fire started and eating a candy bar, I rested about an hour and felt much better. A little sunshine broke through the clouds, and felt so good on my face. I remembered something my dad liked to say, 'When the going gets tough, the tough get going!' Well, I could be tough! After dousing the fire, I started east again as fast as I could walk. The terrain was quite rugged, but I kept going until I just couldn't take another step. By the time I had eaten the last of my jerky and some dry bread, my body just folded up in the blanket and leaned over on the pile of firewood collected for the night. I slept like a log and even forgot to release the safety on the rifle by my side.

"The next morning was fantastic. My socks and shoes had dried by the fire, and felt good until I had walked half an hour through the wet grass. I finished the last of my bread, a hard crust by now, and ran across some ripened salmonberries. Feeling refreshed and renewed, I consulted the map and compass, and headed east once more. By ten o'clock I had walked clear of the alders onto grassy slopes. The fireweed growth was very high, and there were tunnels through it where the bears had roamed in their search for food. Salmonberry bushes grew thickly on the sunny slopes, especially along the small trickles of water I frequently crossed. The eight feet tall elderberry bushes were heavy with shiny red clusters, but I knew they were not tasty right off the plant. The bears must have liked elderberries a lot, because there was plenty of activity in those areas, with large spots of grass and fireweed flattened, perhaps where a bear slept off his orgy of berry feasting!

"I felt I must be getting close to the bay where the lodge was located, but the tall bushes kept me from getting a clear view of much beyond 30 feet ahead. At last I crested a hill and stopped. The bay stretched out in the distance, just a blue finger jutting off the wind streaked Shelikof Strait. I estimated that the bay was about 10 miles away and hurried on. The large size of the bay concerned me; would I be able to see the lodge and know which way to go when I arrived at the beach? I started to sing my way down the slopes, but was too hoarse. After an hour I stopped to take a drink from my canteen. While sitting in the grass I heard the sound of something nearby, a thump, a crack, a grunt, and I slowly rose from my low position to peer over the grass. Thank god, the wind was blowing stiffly in my face, because just about 75 feet away, a huge brown bear was tearing up a large area of earth, pulling plants up by the roots."

Penny gasped, "Oh, my god!" Marie nodded and widened her eyes.

"He was so focused, snorting into the dirt, tossing plants aside. He might have been tearing up some animal's den. I remembered what Dan had said, and kept the rifle ready and backed slowly away, crouched behind the grass. I just hoped he didn't catch my scent or hear me, but with the direction of the wind, it seemed the most logical thing to do. It took an hour to get backed over a little ridge, and when I felt I could stand up, I trotted north in the direction of Shelikof Strait. After half an hour I headed east once more. My knees were shaking and I stumbled many times. My detour around the bear would route me closer to the mouth of the bay.

"It was nearly 5:00 when I stumbled onto the beach. The wind was blowing stiffly from the south, funneling down the bay. Along this stretch of beach, the ground was pretty smooth so I set up a pace heading into the wind. With the pack and rifle bouncing on my back,

I battled the wind gusts, stopping every few minutes to scan the beach for the lodge. After about 45 minutes I saw it, not half a mile away! I had made it! This feeling of excitement came crashing down when I saw the skiff moored in front of the lodge start moving. I could make out two figures in the skiff, and it was heading toward the opposite side of the bay. The wind caused the water to be quite choppy, with large whitecaps obscuring the skiff at times as the person at the controls negotiated through the swells. Fumbling, I let the rifle sling slide off my shoulder, pulled it up, clicked the safety off and fired! When I shot off the second round, the skiff made an arc in the water, and headed for me! Later, it scared me to think I almost missed those fellows, because they were planning to be gone for a week. When I realized I was no longer alone, I sank to the sand."

Penny could stay quiet no longer, so she started clapping and laughing. Her reaction was just the thing needed to lighten the mood, and everyone giggled.

"The old guides were shocked when I told them how far I had come to find them. Having lived in that area for decades, they knew about the archaeologists working on the site. After telling them about Dan's condition, we immediately went to the lodge, and radioed the authorities in Kodiak City. The local flight service was in the air for the rescue before the call ended, and we all realized Dan's life depended on the fastest response possible.

"The two grizzled men, Buck and Harvey, fixed a hot supper of ham steaks with mashed potatoes, and cabbage from their garden. I ate enough to feed two lumberjacks! We sat around the table, drinking Buck's pitch black coffee, waiting to hear word of the rescue. When Harvey asked if I had been working at the site all summer, I told them I was the woman who was reported lost in the plane crash. They had heard about the tragedy of course, and I saw a quizzical look exchanged between them. After explaining how Ivan died, I told them he was the only reason I survived long enough to be found by Dan. Both of the men knew Ivan's grandmother, and said the family would be comforted to hear I considered him a hero. I knew they wondered why I stayed at the lake, but they were too polite to ask. Instead they made much of how I managed to find my way to the bay.

"It was nearly 9 pm when we got the word Dan was just then being flown off Lost Lake! He would be stabilized at the small Kodiak hospital, and flown to Anchorage for surgery the next morning. We three hoorayed and clapped each other's backs."

Penny exclaimed, "At last Mom and I know that you both survived!"

"I was suddenly weak and shaky. Buck prescribed a long soak in their bath house before getting a real night's sleep. He rounded up some clothing left behind by clients, which was heavenly. In a small guest room I sank into the blankets and didn't dream at all.

"Buck was stirring up sourdough griddle cakes when I awoke and made my way to the kitchen. Harvey said he heard from the flight service with a weather report. The winds were too bad between here and Kodiak City for the small plane to pick me up. Maybe they could get to the lodge later in the afternoon. Since I was safe, no risks would be taken. Dan had been flown to Anchorage early that morning and I wanted so desperately to see him. The report on his condition was good, although his recovery would take some time. I can't tell you how relieved I was.

"Buck offered to show me around their lodge and outbuildings. The two-story main house was built of logs, had four bedrooms and a large main room with a stone fireplace. Mounted animal heads and hides adorned the walls everywhere. The large kitchen was furnished with an oil cooking stove, a bigger version of the one at Lost Lake.

The dining area occupied one end of the main room, with a long trestle table and benches. All of this overlooked the bay, magnificent even in the stormy morning. It was obvious that the two men enjoyed the remoteness of their home, sharing it for three decades. They guided for all kinds of Kodiak Island hunts, specializing in trophy brown bears. Clients from all over the world flew in for a first class experience. Framed photos were scattered about, showing movie stars, politicians and world leaders proudly posing with various dead beasts.

"By afternoon we knew that no one would be flying to get me that day. A radioed message about 3:00 confirmed it, and also forwarded the news that my husband had been notified. My stomach knotted, but there had been no way to keep my survival a secret any longer. After dinner, we reclined on the pillowed sofa and chairs in front of a fire. I revealed to Buck and Harvey that after Dan found me, and Ivan died, I was in a fragile state. I told them that Dan was going to walk to the lodge for help, but then I wasn't sure I wanted to go back to my husband and needed time to think.

"Buck's opinion was that Lost Lake was a good spot to think. Harvey seemed less satisfied with my explanation, but accepted it and retrieved a Jim Beam bottle from a cabinet. We three toasted my achievement in surviving almost four days 'bushwhacking,' as Buck put it. In the end, I spent the evening telling stories of how scared I was when I fell in the ravine, and of bears I saw. Buck and Harvey's responses almost turned it into a comedy, and since Dan had survived, I could laugh too.

"The next morning, a small WWII era seaplane called a Widgeon, landed on the bay and tied up at the boat dock. Buck and Harvey insisted they needed to get some supplies in Kodiak City, but I thought at the time they just wanted to take care of me a little longer. We lifted off the bay after gaining speed, skipping along the tops of short waves.

This time in the air, I viewed the forests, lakes, and bays with great interest. I realized more than ever how vast and empty that part of the world is. The engine noise kept us from talking to each other, but we all gestured and pantomimed about what we saw from the small port-hole windows. The plane's hull is like a big metal coffin; I could see the rivets along the seams where the plates meet. The only exits were a trap door above the pilot and a door near the tail. It was very claustrophobic and I was glad the flight would take only 45 minutes. This pilot had also flown the medical crew to pick up Dan. When we boarded the plane, the pilot had given me Dan's small day pack. He explained that Dan instructed him to deliver the pack to me. Before landing in Kodiak City, I opened it and found my journal, the large stone lamp, and a roll of undeveloped film. The pilot also told me that Dan's family was joining him in Anchorage.

"Buck and Harvey checked us into the hotel, and since Ed wouldn't arrive until late afternoon, the two men took me shopping for some nice clothes. I had no money of course, but Harvey turned me over to his niece who worked for Alaska Commercial Company. Adele helped me choose a pair of navy slacks with a feminine white crepe blouse, navy and red embroidery adorning the collar and long sleeved cuffs. Buck insisted I needed a short gabardine jacket, and I chose one of soft gray. New underwear, navy low heeled shoes and a red shoulder bag completed the outfit. After Buck paid for the clothes, he informed me that Harvey had made an appointment with the hair salon across the street, so I could look like a movie star! By the time my hair was cut in the new pixie style, and new makeup purchased, I felt like Cinderella!

"Back at the hotel, I moved the things from Dan's day pack into my new bag, and then prepared myself to see Ed. Practicing how I would tell him I was filing for a divorce when we returned to Seattle, my hands started shaking. I needed some help, so I knocked on Buck's door, and asked if he had any Jim Beam in his room. Of course he did, and we had a nip, which warmed my belly, and calmed my nerves. That was the last hard liquor I ever drank. Harvey joined us and both men declared I was absolutely beautiful, which made me feel great."

Rosalie observed out loud, "It seems that Buck and Harvey really took you under their wings. They must have been awfully nice men."

Marie answered, "Absolutely the best! I stayed in contact with them until they passed away in the 1960's. Since neither one had children, they accumulated many adoring nieces, nephews and just plain friends. Hmm … what do you say to a pot of coffee?"

The coffee was a strong blend but served with real cream to remove any bitterness. Marie told the women about her children; her son Chris, who is the curator for a Native American museum, and his wife live nearby. Their two daughters are attending college. Marie's daughter Louisa followed in her mother's footsteps, illustrating children's books. She lives in Seattle with her husband. It was clear that Marie loved her family very much.

Penny begged Marie to continue with her story, and so she did.

"The three of us took a taxi to the airport, and were met there by several reporters, some from Anchorage and even one from Seattle. Ed emerged from the plane a bit rumpled, but immediately realized there were reporters with flash bulbs popping, so he straightened his tie, smiled and waved. Descending the ramp steps, he scanned the crowd, not noticing that I was standing just a few feet from him. I took such delight in this, and stepped up to him, saying "I guess you are surprised." His mouth dropped open, and he tried to speak but only managed to look like a guppy in a fishbowl. After the initial shock of how I looked, he made a big pretense of being overjoyed to find out I was alive. After a few photos were taken, we joined Harvey and Buck in the taxi. I was so relieved they were with us, because I could tell that Ed was seething beneath his gallant exterior.

"Alone in our hotel room, Ed raged at me, saying he looked like a fool grieving over me while I played this hide and seek game. He was so angry about the weeks I spent with another man, but he didn't seem to care about my brush with death, nor was he proud of my harrowing walk. I knew he wouldn't hit me now, because we were to join a group in the hotel restaurant later. Ed spat that he could tell I thought I was so smart, and demanded to know who paid for my clothes and salon visit. Spitefully, he sneered and insinuated I was a kept woman, but he would make sure the 'old codgers' were paid back. I was embarrassed knowing the hotel walls were thin, and people in nearby rooms could overhear his remarks. Ed was already affecting my self-confidence by the time we joined the others for dinner.

"As we sat down at our corner table alone, Ed wordlessly tossed some bills on Harvey and Buck's table. I couldn't meet their eyes, but a few minutes later I looked their way to see them frowning and in a quiet huddle. I think they heard Ed's rant in the room, and were beginning to understand why I had delayed going back to Seattle. But I felt very alone and scared, not knowing how I would tell Ed I wanted a divorce. If I could get away from him, I wouldn't even care that it appeared he was raiding my parents' money, judging from the roll of bills he pulled out to pay for my clothes. We ordered dinner, and I tried to be cheerful in the public eye. Ed kept prodding for details, whispering that I disgraced him, and threatening he would teach me a lesson when we got home. I began perspiring; a bead of sweat ran from my hairline down my temple. Ed saw it, chuckled and reached out with a finger to trace its route. His hand dropped to my arm and put a vice hold around my elbow. I couldn't move, so afraid I was of his wrath. Suddenly, Buck got up from his seat and stood by our table. He smiled broadly and began telling Ed how extraordinary I was, walking through such dangerous territory alone. Then he leaned down, met my eyes, and said "Well, now you don't EVER have to be afraid of ANYTHING or ANYBODY again!" Buck straightened up and smiled again, as Ed gave me his usual 'I'll take care of you later' look.

"Sensing that Buck was going to jerk Ed out of his chair, I thought 'Buck is right!' Just as Ed started to meanly pinch my leg under the tablecloth I rose, grabbed my bag and used all my strength to strike him across the face with it. The stone lamp in the bag hit him so hard it forced his chair to tip over onto the floor. While he was still dazed, I stood over him with arm raised and said for all to hear, 'Ed, I am through with you! If you ever lay a hand on me again, I will shoot you between the eyes and don't think I won't!' Buck and Harvey laughed as confused diners looked on. Harvey whispered for me to leave and they would take care of Ed. I retreated to my room, and barred the door. Later, when I opened it for Buck, he said they would make sure Ed missed the flight back to Seattle the next morning to give me a head start. I planted a kiss on his cheek, and thanked him for everything. I found out they took him to the bar and got him very drunk. When I caught the dawn flight, Ed was sleeping it off in Harvey's room.

Penny could not hold her enthusiasm, saying "I would have liked to see you conk Ed with that purse!" The three women laughed at the thought of Ed spread out on the floor.

"I arrived in Seattle mid-day, took a taxi straight to the bank, and withdrew what was left of the money. I walked across the street to a different bank and opened a checking account in my name only. Later I checked into a small hotel and paid in advance for a week's stay. The next morning it took me just an hour to gather up what

69

I wanted from the house, which wasn't much. Most of my clothes were too big, but I wanted some of the things that were left to me by my parents, such as Mom's silver service. After the taxi driver helped carry the boxes to my hotel room, I sat on the bed and sadly looked at what was left of six years with Ed. Then I thought, what am I sad about? I would see an attorney, and start over. I admitted that my new life could not be with Dan. I told myself that we had been wrong to give in to romantic feelings when we should have thought of others. I would treasure the time we had together and remember him forever. He helped me rediscover myself.

"A few days later in a department store I ran into Mildred, the librarian. This time I didn't avoid her. She had read of my survival and wanted to hear the whole story from beginning to end. We ended up visiting a long time over coffee at her house. I told her why I had acted strangely at the library those months, but the rest of my story would take many more cups of coffee the following day, as I revealed what happened on Kodiak Island. Mildred was a WWII widow living alone, and she suggested I move out of the hotel into her spare bedroom. I agreed, only if I paid a fair rent, which was still less than the hotel, and I wouldn't have to eat all my meals out. The money I had would last a few months, but I still needed to find a job. I discovered that Ed lost his job with the auto dealership. My attorney said it would take several months to complete the divorce proceedings, but he had gathered information about Ed's unfaithfulness, so his own habits expedited the paperwork. Mildred became a dear friend, very much a part of my life for the next thirty years. I found a part time job selling stationary supplies at Nordstrom and volunteered at the library, so my mind was kept busy. I thought of Dan every evening, especially when the stars appeared and on days when fog thickly swirled in from the waterfront. The roll of film I found in the back pack was developed, and I kept the photos in the nightstand. They showed two people having a great time, very proud of the cave discovery.

"A few days before Christmas Mildred asked if I could drop some books off for her at one of the downtown hotels. The Puget Palace Hotel was old but the lobby was tidy. The desk clerk was a friend of Mildred's so we talked a bit. Suddenly two old gents swooped up to me exclaiming, 'Here's Marie!' and 'We've been tryin' to find you!' Buck, Harvey and I sat in the little hotel bar for an hour, rehashing my journey from Lost Lake to their lodge, and how they detained Ed the day I left. I delighted in telling them of my upcoming divorce. Harvey asked frankly if Dan and I would be getting together. I told them that since he had a wife and child, I had to give up that part of my dream. They looked at each other with confusion, and told me about Dan's family. His mother and sister had flown from Oregon to see him in the hospital. His wife and son died during WWII. My heart just stopped. I realized what he wanted to tell me before I left that day."

"Oh, my gosh", Rosalie murmured.

"Buck told me how Dan and his wife met in college, and married right after he graduated. After one more year of graduate school in Fairbanks, Dan became the father of an adored son. The war started and Dan enlisted. He was sent overseas very soon after basic training, and Lillian, whose home was on Atka Island in the Aleutians, took their son back there to live with her grandmother. Lillian's mother was an Aleut native, who had married a white school teacher, but both died of typhoid fever when she was small.

"When the Japanese became a threat in the Aleutians, our government decided it was in the best interest to evacuate all the islands. Instead of returning to Fairbanks as she could have done, Lillian and her son accompanied her grandmother and other relatives to an internment camp in southeast Alaska. It was set up in an abandoned cannery, with primitive facilities, and soon various illnesses struck the vulnerable population. Both Lillian and Johnny died of complications of measles. Dan did not get notification until three months later. After the war he returned to Fairbanks, and buried himself in his studies, finished a graduate degree and became an associate professor of archaeology a couple of years later. It was said that he seldom spoke of his wife and son.

"Buck said they heard Dan had tried to find me, had written to the address he copied from my journal; however, the letters were returned since I couldn't leave a forwarding address, fearing that Ed would somehow find me. I couldn't believe my ears! Hugging both of the old guides, I quickly returned to the library to tell Mildred the news. She said there was only one thing to do and that was to fly to Fairbanks. First I called the college to make sure Dan was teaching that semester, after the surgeries on his leg. The department secretary said he was in class, but I could leave a message. I declined, wanting instead to see his face, which would tell me if he still felt about me, the way I felt about him.

"The weather was very cold in Fairbanks of course, dipping to minus 40 degrees many nights; however, Mildred packed me off with winter gear worthy of an Eskimo. She was giddy with excitement, and I promised I would call her soon to let her know what happened.

"Two days later, about midnight I landed in Fairbanks. I didn't know where Dan lived, so I had to stay in a hotel until the next morning. When I found his department on the campus, I was told he was in class. I replied that I had a delivery for him and would wait. A few minutes later the secretary walked down the hall, and I slipped through the unlocked door that had his name on it. Taking the stone lamp from my bag, I set it in the middle of his desk. Suddenly I heard Dan's voice asking the secretary for any messages or appointments scheduled in the afternoon. Evidently this was the last day of classes before Christmas break because the lady asked if he was going out of town for the holidays. He replied that he was flying to Seattle to look up a friend. The secretary said, 'A young lady was here with a delivery, but she must have left.' Dan responded that he wasn't expecting anything, and wondered what it could be. His voice became clearer and I realized he was approaching his office, so I quickly stepped over to the wall that would be hidden when he opened the door. He entered, walking with a pronounced limp and using a cane, as he read through his messages. Dan stood by his desk, and it took a moment for him to realize there was something out of order there. He glanced at the desk, looked up, then focused on the desk again before picking up the stone lamp. Hurrying to the window that overlooked the commons area outside the science building, he murmured, 'Marie.'

"I waited half a beat, and answered, 'I am here.' Dan turned slowly. Later he told me he thought he was hearing things and was afraid to look around, afraid I wasn't really there! When I saw his face I said, 'Ed is out of my life and I know what you wanted to tell me.' He reached for me. We were seldom apart during almost sixty years of marriage."

Penny gave a big sniff, and then she noticed that her mom had tears streaming down her cheeks. Marie's eyes also were misty. When she saw that Penny noticed, Marie said, "I love telling our story!" They all laughed, blew noses, and dabbed eyes.

Marie said, "Penny, could you step into the living room please, and look on the bottom shelf of the corner bookcase. Bring us one of the large archaeology books and I'll show you something. When Penny returned with the book, Marie pointed to the title and author: *Petroglyphs of the Alaska Peninsula by Dan Moore.* The dust jacket's rear cover featured a photo of an archaeological site. A handsome man wearing a plaid shirt was pointing to a slab of decorated rock for a slim young woman to inspect. The photographer must have said "Look here!" since they both were smiling right at the camera. A young boy stood at the man's side, looking up at him. The caption under the photo read *Author Dan Moore and Illustrator Marie Hill Moore with their son Chris, Chignik Bay site, August 1958.*

"What a happy ending!" Penny chirped.

Rosalie asked, "So you became an illustrator of his discoveries?"

"First I returned to college to finish my art degree. Chris was born on the day I graduated. In 1960 our daughter, Louisa, was born. The four of us spent every summer in the field together, until the children left home. To answer your question: yes, I was his illustrator. He wouldn't allow anyone else. I also did some illustrating for children's books, but now days I can't do much sketching since my hands aren't very steady."

"Knock, knock! Hey, Mom, are you out back?" A tall man with a shy smile appeared in the kitchen door. After introductions were made, Chris told Rosalie and Penny how excited his mother had been when she heard the journal was safe.

Rosalie said, "Actually, my husband is the one who thought of calling the auction company, to track Marie down."

"That reminds me, I have something for you and Penny. I'll be right back," and Marie disappeared into the house.

"I'll have to say, at first we thought the journal was fiction, a story someone was making up," Penny admitted.

Chris nodded, "Every time we have a family gathering, someone asks her to tell how she and Dad met, one more time. Most of us know the story by heart, but I never get tired of hearing it. Mom is a pretty remarkable woman, and Dad idolized her. They each felt the other one made life worth living. Dad passed away just two years ago, and I'm sure she still talks to him every day."

Penny said, "I think she is a lucky woman."

"They never forgot the boy who helped her survive until Dad found them. I can't forget him either, since my middle name is Ivan! You know, they stayed in contact with Ivan's mother until she passed away."

Rosalie asked, "What happened to Tom?"

" Tom taught in that village for four more years. He moved to the Warm Springs Reservation near Mt. Hood and taught there until he retired. During that time he remarried, and their sons are considered our cousins, great guys.

Marie returned to the patio with two small framed prints.

"I want you to have something for the trouble you took to find me. I hope you like them."

Rosalie held a sketch depicting a crude human figure with a spear. Penny's sketch featured two stylized seals, and both sketches were labeled Lost Lake Cave, 1950. Both women were overwhelmed with the gifts, but Marie insisted that they have the sketches. She told them more about the cave, and their work the next summer to finish documenting all of the drawings.

While the women were chatting, Chris was working somewhere in the apartment, then appeared at the kitchen door again.

"Ok, Mom, I finally remembered to bring my power screwdriver. The print you wanted hung in the bedroom is up. Come take a look."

They all filed into the pleasantly furnished room, where Marie declared the print was right where she wanted, hung on the wall just beyond the foot of her bed. Marie was sitting on the edge of her bed, suddenly very quiet.

"I'm feeling a bit shaky, Chris. I think I need to lie down for little while."

Chris asked, "Do you need your medicine?"

Marie assured him that all she needed was a little nap before dinner, and turned to Penny and Rosalie.

"Can you come back to visit me again soon? I would love to hear about your families."

"Of course! I'll call you in a few days." Rosalie replied. "I hope we didn't tire you out."

Marie gestured for them to come closer so she could give each woman a warm hug. "Your visit means a lot to me. Thank you for caring so much." Chris spread a quilt over his mother before they stepped into the hall.

"Don't worry, she'll be ok. Mom is just wearing out. I can tell you though, she is very happy today."

Rosalie took one more look at the figure on the bed, slightly propped up with pillows. Marie was smiling at the newly hung sketch; the stone lamp was frozen in time, holding memories for her to dream about. On her bedside table in front of a framed photo of Dan and Marie, lay the little leather journal.

Lonely Prairie

Rummaging in the bottom desk drawer, Rosalie Evans was quickly becoming annoyed with herself for misplacing a particular antique book. The little diary was the whole reason for her trip to Dallas, and now she couldn't find it. Thinking that she must have taken it home, Rosalie closed the book shop early, and taped a note on the door advising customers that Driftwood Books would be closed until the next week.

Rosalie searched her canvas tote bag for the car keys, and found the missing diary. "Oh, yes," she chuckled, "That was where I put it for safe keeping." She couldn't resist opening the tattered volume to read the first entry once again.

15 June 1860
Dear Diary,
Today is my birthday. I am fourteen years old. Mother says fourteen is the age when young ladies begin writing in diaries. My older sister Leticia has been writing in hers for two years. Mother quilted a beautiful cover for mine with flowers of many colors embroidered around the edges and my name in the middle. I will keep it forever. I live in Bellville, Missouri, and I have three brothers and three sisters. My parents are Thomas and Martha Lee. We live on a farm and Father teaches school in the winters. Gramps and Granny Lee live on their

own farm nearby. Mother is the most beautiful mother in town, and she is very good. I want to be just like her when I grow up. Mother says I have an olive complexion like hers. My hair is not as curly, but it is very black. Mother is so small that she cannot see over Father's shoulder. I was named for her sister, Susan, and Father's sister, Anne. I love the outdoors and dislike doing household chores. My parents believe there is going to be a war between states in the south, and states in the north.

Closing the diary to more closely examine the quilted covers, Rosalie could just make out *SU*. Only a portion of the embroidered flowers remained, and cotton batting showed at the corners where the aged muslin fabric was worn through. Small script filled both sides of the pages, with most entries in ink. Rosalie tucked the diary back in her bag, and headed home to pack for her trip. Her cousin Mary was a genealogy researcher in Dallas, so Rosalie was using that excuse to visit. She had scanned through the diary enough to realize it should be returned to the author's descendants, who might be in Texas. Rosalie and Mary were planning to scour public records to research the diary, which appeared to span thirty years.

This small book of memories had been in the bottom drawer of Rosalie's desk at the book shop for quite some time; she couldn't remember exactly when or where she acquired it. Anything personal, such as diaries or letters, found with used books Rosalie purchased for her shop's inventory, were deposited in the drawer until she had time to look for clues that might lead to owners or relatives.

The next morning, after checking in at the airline counter and locating her gate, Rosalie retrieved the diary to resume reading Susan's story. The tattered first page of the diary had been glued inside the front cover, probably because it had become detached at some point. At the very top of that page, a young hand had carefully written "Susan Anne Lee."

3 October 1860

Dear Diary,

Mother says I need more practice making my stitching neater. She gave me some handkerchief squares to hem and embroider for Granny Lee. I love Granny but her eyes are sharp as a hawk's. She will find any mistakes I make, faster than Mother. Father and the boys found a bee's hive in a hickory tree near the river. Father smoked the bees to make gathering their honey easier, but James and Tommy came home with several stings already daubed with mud poultices. I wanted to help get the honey but Mother said that wouldn't be lady-like, and besides, Leticia and I had to help do a big washing which took most of the day.

5 October 1860

Dear Diary,

After church all of our neighbors got together at the pond near the Brown's farm for a picnic. My best friend is Rachel Brown. She has an older brother, Mason. Mother allowed us girls to wade along the pond's edge, but of course the boys got wet all over. Sometimes I wish I was a boy! I ate too much chocolate cake and now I have a stomach ache.

10 October 1860

Dear Diary,

Our church had an autumn bazaar, and Granny made pies and breads to sell. Mother finished four lace collars and Leticia made three aprons. I sewed ribbons onto three small hair combs Mother gave me. The money collected from selling everything went into the church building fund. Father butchered a hog with all our help. Gramps hurt his back while moving tables at the bazaar, and couldn't come. Tommy is only ten years old but he and James helped with the cleaning and carving up parts. Leticia and I helped Mother render the lard by taking turns at stirring and keeping the dogs away. Cora was in charge of the twins, Grace and Henry, who are just two years old and a lot of trouble. Father is preparing meat for the smokehouse while Mother is making sausage.

14 October 1860
Dear Diary,
Rachel came today, riding along in the wagon with her brother when he asked to borrow Father's large whipsaw. She stayed all day, and helped Mother and I make apple butter. Rachel and I have been best friends for a long time. Although she dislikes her copper colored, hair, I think it's beautiful. Leticia and I walked Rachel home after supper. I think my sister is being forward with Rachel's brother, but he does not seem to mind. She laughs at just about anything he says. Right now the rain is pounding on the roof just above my head, which probably means we will not be washing clothes tomorrow.

16 October 1860
Dear Diary,
It is very late and the little candle is sputtering. Mother let me have a day to myself with no chores. She thought I might go see Rachel, but I wanted to be alone. It is hard to find a place and time where no big or little voices are pecking at my thoughts. I walked across the meadow to climb the rocky mound where I like to watch the clouds. When I lay down among the gray boulders, all the world was blocked out. With only the sounds of the wind in my head, I felt as if I was floating on one of the clouds. Mother, Leticia, and I have been working late in the evenings, sewing new winter dresses. I chose

a dark blue and brown plaid material. The style is fitted at the waist, but with a short peplum, and white lace inset at the throat and cuffs. Leticia chose narrow stripes of dark and light brown, styled like mine. Cora's is a dark blue material with tiny white bouquets all over. Her skirts are still short, but only for another year or two. Cora's stitches are not very tiny, so we just let her hem the dresses. Granny is making each of us new white petticoats and drawers.

30 October 1860
Dear Diary,

I spent all morning ironing our dresses for the barn dance tomorrow night. Mother made several pies and cakes, and the men will cook a passel of wild turkeys and a side of venison on spits. Granny is bringing her famous green tomato chutney and pickled watermelon. I can't wait to see Rachel's new dress. School begins on Monday!

1 November 1860
Dear Diary,

After church Leticia and I walked home with Rachel and Mason. Later, Leticia told me that Mason said if Abraham Lincoln is elected president, there will certainly be a war. Father doesn't believe in men enslaving other human beings, and he told us Mister Lincoln will try to change the laws so plantation owners have to free their slaves and pay wages to their farm workers. We don't know anyone who has slaves in Bellville, but when Father and Mother first married in Virginia, they knew of many slave owners. In our history lessons we have studied about wars that ruined countries and killed thousands of people, so I am really scared.

7 November 1860

Dear Diary,

Leticia helped Mother make soap on Saturday, while I ironed dresses and shirts. I can't get the ruffles ironed pretty like Mother. I love school. We are so lucky to have Father as a teacher. He and Mother believe that girls need to be educated, as much as boys. Many families don't send any of their children to school. Reading is my favorite subject. Father has sixteen pupils this winter, too many for our house so he is using the Methodist Church in town. James is finished with his schooling, so he takes care of the farm. Our school day ends at two o'clock which gives Father time to help James before it is too dark. A new family, the Bakers, purchased the old Winthrop farm and three of their children are Father's students. The two oldest boys help with the farm; I think their names are Josh and T.J.

15 December 1860

Dear Diary,

Mr. Lincoln has been elected president! Mother cried when we got the news. South Carolina threatens to withdraw from being part of the United States. Father says it's called secede when this happens, and if they do, other states will follow. I try to not worry about it. Leticia and Mason are sweethearts, I believe. He comes over on Saturday evenings and after church on Sundays. Although he spends a lot of time talking to Father, his eyes are on Leticia. Before he leaves for home, they spend a long time talking at the gate. I heard Granny say to Mother they make a nice couple. Mason is rather handsome, and when he stands next to our Leticia they both have sparkly looks in their eyes. My sister's dark hair, curly like Mother's, explodes from her net forming corkscrews along the sides of her face. Once I saw Mason stroke her curls as they shared a private moment. I think that is what love looks like.

The Portland to Dallas flight boarded, and as the plane took off, Rosalie was thinking about Susan's mother crying over the news of Lincoln's election. Was she crying with joy because Lincoln was elected, or upset with the thought there would be a war?

25 December 1860
Dear Diary,

We invited the Baker and Brown families for Christmas dinner, along with Granny and Gramps, and the new snow made it a perfect day. We children sang carols and soon our parents joined in. Leticia, Cora, Rachel and I played games with the younger children, and then Father gave oranges and peppermint sticks to everyone. Josh and T.J. Baker took all the young people for a fast ride in their sleigh across the pasture, over the hill toward the river. Tonight Leticia showed me a gift that Mason secretly gave her. He had whittled on a small tree burl until it looks just like a bowl with a fitted lid. Burnt into the underside of the lid were their initials. Leticia says she will use it to hold her only piece of Sunday jewelry, the silver chain and locket Granny Lee gave her.

11 March 1861
Dear Diary,

Just as we thought spring was coming, the weather turned very cold. Instead of rain, we got sleet which coated everything. Leticia fell and sprang her wrist when she walking back from the chicken coop. Cora and I are hooking a rug with rags Granny gave us.

20 April 1861
Dear Diary,

Father rode to Clinton where he managed to get more news about the Union. He was very sad when he got home having to tell us that several states have seceded and war has begun. Missouri will not secede, even though some landowners have slaves. James wants to join the Union army, but it upset Mother so much, he promised he would wait for now. Josh Baker came over to talk with Father about the war. Josh's father and brother support the Confederacy, and this upsets Josh very much. While they talked, I sat still as a mouse on the stairs and listened. Mother invited Josh, T.J., Mason and Rachel for supper tomorrow evening, to help us celebrate Leticia's graduation from school. When James graduated, Father bought him a pocket watch, and had it engraved. For Leticia, he purchased a locket and chain, with similar engraving.

15 June 1861
Dear Diary,
Another birthday has come and gone. So much happened this year that I feel a lot older. Leticia told me she and Mason have promised themselves to each other. She is seventeen and he is eighteen, so I am sure they will have to wait at least two years before Father will allow them to marry. My sister Cora has been very sick with the mumps, but improved over the last week. I spend many hours sitting by her bedside, reading when she feels like listening. Mother is so brave when the children are ill, with her calm attitude giving us all a hopeful feeling. Our family is working very hard, clearing more fields to plant since Father says feeding and clothing the soldiers will put a demand on goods. Mother says we will put up more fruits and vegetables this year, and James even dug another root cellar to hold sweet potatoes and onions. Our plow horse is lame, so Father is trading some harness work for a sturdy mule the blacksmith owns. Several men have gone off to fight the confederates. A few, like Josh's brother T.J., have joined the south's army. Mrs. Baker organized a

ladies' group that makes bandages for the wounded. Leticia, Rachel and I join them at the church every Wednesday afternoon, along with our mothers. We feel sorry for Mrs. Baker, having one son fighting for the Confederates, and another son wanting to join the Union troops.

30 July 1861
Dear Diary,

Josh Baker spends several evenings a week here. I think he values Father's opinion on the war since he talks over the news we get from the battlefronts with James and Father. Sometimes he comes early while I am milking Bossy, and carries the bucket to the house. Little Henry and Grace climb all over Josh, begging for a ride on his back. I was pleased to hear that Josh is well educated and he told me his mother encourages him to continue with studies even though his formal schooling is over. Today Mother made sauerkraut. Leticia and I got the cabbage and onions sliced and in the brown crock, while Mother fixed the brine. Tommy was enlisted to pound the cabbage down after each layer. After six weeks Mother will check it for readiness. It makes the storeroom smell so sharp that it makes my eyes water. I don't like sauerkraut but have to eat some since Mother says it keeps us healthier. The war wears on, with more men leaving home to fight. Most join the Union troops, but a few continue to join the Confederates.

22 August 1861
Dear Diary,

Our harvests are bountiful, so the root cellars are filling up. Father sold a wagonload of sweet potatoes and corn to an army post in Clinton. Mother sends all of us to pick berries every day, since she is busy making preserves and jellies. The wild plums are just ripening, which is my favorite fruit for jams. Father promised us girls that we could have the surplus honey he and Tommy gathered last week, after Mother stored what she needed. Leticia, Cora and I traded it to the general store for some much needed dress making goods. Josh, James, and Mason still talk seriously of joining in the fight. Some families have already been notified of their loved one's death or injury. There's been no word from T.J. since he was sent to Boonville over two months ago. We heard that the Confederates were beaten in a battle there. I climbed the rocky mound across the pasture this afternoon, and stretched out in the sun. By shading my eyes I could watch the few clouds as they made dark shapes on the fields. A squirrel dodged in and out of the rocks, joyfully stowing food in his cache. As silly as it sounds, I felt envious of his carefree life. We have so much to worry about.

12 September 1861
Dear Diary,
Rachel and Mason came over today with the news about T.J. Baker. He was badly wounded in Boonville, and lost his right leg below the knee. Mr. Baker and Josh are taking the wagon to bring him back home for the family to nurse. What a terrible thing to happen. Leticia is so afraid Mason will get killed if he goes to fight and she wants so much for them to be married. Mother was summoned late last night to help a young couple birth their baby. The doctor is gone, sewing up soldiers for the Union.

28 October 1861
Dear Diary,
Rachel's father is just recovering from a lung ailment, so James is helping Mason with their farm work this week. Josh also helps out some days. I took a basket of fried chicken to them this evening,

and later Josh brought me home in the wagon. Since it was too cold to visit outside, we sat by the kitchen stove awhile. Josh is awfully sweet and good looking; his light brown hair is worn a bit longer than James wears his. He is taller than Father and just told me he is nineteen years old.

14 December 1861
Dear Diary

To get our minds off the war Father bought a copy of Charles Dickens' *A Christmas Carol,* so Leticia and I take turns reading it to the family after supper.

28 December 1861
Dear Diary,

All of our friends and neighbors are trying to keep up their spirits, so we have eaten and sung through several holiday parties. Josh and I attended most of them together, along with Leticia and Mason. There is no talk about us being a couple of course, since I am too young to have a beau, according to Father. Josh and I do have a wonderful time together, agreeing on most everything important in the world. I behaved boldly and gave Josh a lock of my hair, braided for a bookmark. He gave me his school spelling medal, and told me something important that I cannot share with anyone yet.

3 January 1862
Dear Diary,

I no longer have to keep a secret. Mason, James and Josh have announced to the families that they are joining the Union Army. After Mason and Josh told their families, they came to our house tonight to be with James when he told Mother and Father of their decisions.

Tommy is happy to have a soldier brother, but Cora is sad James will not be around to tease her. I felt a little guilty that I already knew, but I think Leticia did too. Mother cried at first, but she knew there was nothing she could say to James that would change his mind. Leticia and Mason said they were going for a ride in the sled, and invited Josh and me. Father couldn't deny the boys anything, so off we went! I will remember this night forever. Josh held me close under the robe, and kissed me sweetly one time. I never dreamed that kissing was such a wondrous experience. I couldn't breathe for a minute, and I wanted to cry and kiss him back. I understand now why Leticia has been so upset with the thought of Mason leaving, as I feel the same about Josh.

16 January 1862
Dear Diary,

Mason Brown, Josh Baker, and our James left last week for Jefferson City, but we do not know where they will be posted. Leticia cried for two days after Mason left. They told everyone of their commitment, and Father gave his blessing and permission to marry when the war ends. I am so happy for them. There has been a skirmish near Bellville, and Father says we girls must not walk anywhere alone. Livestock has been stolen from several farms, including Mr. Brown's milk cow. Father and Gramps predict that the Rebels will be beaten soon. I have heard them talk about how few factories there are in the south, and that the Union troops are blockading ports to prevent European ships from bringing supplies to the Rebels.

February 1862
Dear Diary,

I have been thinking of Mother, ever so hard. She is so sad for James to be gone and in such danger. Mother is so very close to us all, as if her children are what make her draw a breath. It was strange that she never spoke of her own mother or father, but now I understand. I knew she had a sister, Susan, since I am named for her. Leticia and I asked Mother about her family, and she told us she could remember a few things; it is such a sad story. Her father, Robert Mitchell, was a farmer in Tennessee, but he died when Mother was four years old. The farm had been mortgaged, so the bank took it a few months later, and her father's will granted his slaves their freedom. Grandmother Sally and Mother then lived with relatives in Alabama, where Grandmother had to take in sewing. Grandmother later married a teamster named Cooper, and had another daughter, my Aunt Susan. After Mother turned twelve years old, a local merchant offered to send her to Richmond, Virginia, to live with his sister's family, and be educated at a girls' school, since Grandmother and her husband had no means of doing so. Instead of sending her to school, the family used Mother as a servant. She was terribly mistreated and ran away two years later. Granny Lee saw her in town begging for food, and took her home. They were never able to locate her family in Alabama, so Mother stayed with the Lee's. Five years later, Mother married Granny Lee's youngest son, Thomas, my father. Leticia and I hugged Mother, and told her we love her so much. I also told her I was so sorry she did not ever get to see her mother again. I cannot imagine the pain of being separated from my parents like that. I don't know if I will ever be able to move away, even when I get married.

3 March 1862
Dear Diary,

I begged Mother to let me make a split riding skirt so I can ride my horse astride instead of side-saddle. Rachel has ridden astride for two years. After consulting Father, Mother agreed to it but only on the farm, not in public.

4 April 1862
Dear Diary,

We heard of a terrible battle at Pea Ridge, where many soldiers were killed or maimed. We pray our men are safe. I don't understand why men fight each other to the death, when there must be a better solution to their differences. To think of Americans fighting each other, when once they were friends, is just so terrible. I have been writing to James and Josh, and it seems that they do get my letters most of the time. Mother said that they would like to hear how things are going at home, so I write only the good news. I told James about Henry getting butted by a goat so hard he couldn't sit down for two days, and the story about Tommy when he tried to chase off a skunk, and got sprayed so bad he couldn't sleep in the house for two nights! I could just imagine James laughing as he read it. Leticia and I knitted mittens and scarves for our soldiers this winter and sent the box with a soldier in their company, who had come home for his mother's burial. Josh wrote me that the mittens were very welcome, and he was sure his ears would have frozen off without the scarf. I wrote Josh about the spring planting, and wild turkeys Father shot last week. During school this winter, Father tacked a large map of the United States on the wall, and showed the students where different battles took place. I don't believe Mr. Baker lets his wife write to Josh very often, so I do! I do not tell him that T.J. is very withdrawn, but I can say he gets around with a crutch now. The Baker's younger children did not attend school this winter, and I don't know why.

18 July 1862
Dear Diary,

Rachel and I have been riding our horses down to the river at least twice a week this summer. When we are certain that no one can see us, we release our hair from the nets to let it stream behind us as we bolt across the meadow. Mother would not like it, but Rachel and I are sixteen now and see no harm in a little freedom.

17 September 1862

We have received such terrible news. My brave brother was killed in a battle at Lone Jack, when the Rebels overran their company. Mother blames herself for letting James join up, but after one night of inconsolable grieving, she has returned to making sure the remainder of the family is comforted. After the battle and retreat, Josh and Mason were granted a short leave, so they delivered the Captain's letter to Mother and Father. Father is very quiet today, but several neighbor men came to the house this evening. They all sat on the porch, talking about what a nice young man James was, and how he will be remembered for his good heart and hard work. Some of these men have already lost members of their own families. Mrs. Baker and Mason's mother, Mrs. Brown, stayed with us today, quietly talking and sewing. Leticia, Cora and I have cried all the tears we can. The twins are too young to understand, but Tommy just sits by Father's side, listening to the men talk about James. Mason and Josh have only three days at home. Mother allowed Leticia to stay at the Brown's, so they could be together as much as possible. Rachel came to stay with us so Leticia can have her room. Mother knows that Mrs. Brown will see that everything is proper. The neighboring men prodded Josh for details of the battle, but he did not satisfy their curiosity. He would only say that it was a slaughter, and James was a hero.

Rosalie sipped the hot coffee placed on her tray, and thought of Martha Lee's grief on hearing of her son's death. Rosalie decided that her earlier reaction to Lincoln's election was for the lives she knew would be lost in the conflict to follow. Even then, women probably thought that if mothers ran the world, there would be no wars. Rosalie noticed that Susan no longer began her entries with "dear diary."

26 September 1862

The last evening Josh was home, we sat in the orchard and talked for hours about what the future would hold for us and our families when the war ends. Josh said he knows I am young, but he would like to think I will wait for him, and not do anything foolish with another fellow while he is gone. It wasn't quite a proposal, but those were beautiful words to me, and I promised I would not be foolish! Josh then kissed me so deeply, I thought I would swoon. We both were shaking and wanted each other so much, but Josh pushed away from me, saying we needed to talk about something else. He was right! He is so troubled about his family. The Baker's are being torn apart with T.J. and his father so certain the Rebels will win the war. Many folks around here will not speak to them. I heard Mrs. Baker tell Mother that her husband ordered her to stay home and not visit with the neighbors. She said she would not obey him, but I believe she is afraid to come see us very often. Mother sends Leticia and me to their farm every few days, to exchange news of the war and visit awhile with her. Josh's brother, T.J., only scowls when we greet him.

23 December 1862

After months of struggling to accept James' death, we just found out that Josh and Mason are in a prisoner-of-war camp in Louisiana. Mrs. Brown got a note from Mason, saying their squad was captured while crossing a river. They are uninjured, although there is little to eat. She is going to arrange to get a box of food to him. Mrs. Baker will also send a box to Josh, and we all pray that at least one reaches them.

We are all so worried, and hope there will be a prisoner exchange to set them free soon. There have been several raids and skirmishes in the county, and some caused damage in Bellville.

8 May 1863

We had not heard from our men since Christmas, when Mrs. Baker received a letter saying they have been shipped to a camp in Mississippi. A doctor, who is allowed to visit the camp occasionally, smuggles out messages to families, for which we are truly grateful. Everyone is so worried about them, since we have heard how wretched the camps are. We will try to send them food and clothing; however, everyone's own clothes are worn, and hard to replace. We have to make do with our old dresses and shirts. Father mends the shoes and boots as good as he can, but he cannot make new ones for growing feet. Union and Confederate troops are fighting all around us. Some towns have been pillaged and even completely burned down. A farmer near Bellville was killed last week, while trying to prevent his horses from being stolen. A few more families around here have loved ones coming home, thankfully alive, but some are terribly maimed. It seems that the only young men we have in town now are blind, missing limbs, or have shattered nerves. Will Josh and Mason be whole when this war is over?

1 August 1863

There was an awful battle near Gettysburg, Pennsylvania. Thousands of lives were lost on both sides, but the Union forces beat down Lee. Two families here lost sons who were fighting for the Union, and one father got word his Confederate soldier son was killed. There have been no messages from Josh or Mason. Mother invited several ladies to a quilting bee at our house. When she lowered the frame from the parlor ceiling and placed chairs all around, the whole room was stuffed, wall to wall. The quilt is for the Lovett's youngest daughter Paulina, who is getting married next month. At times when I am feeling especially sad, I think about my own wedding someday. Josh is in my thoughts, day and night.

2 October 1863

Mrs. Baker came to our house in a hurry this morning to show us a message she got from Josh. He and Mason escaped from the prison camp! She had hidden money in a sack of dried peaches smuggled to them, and they used that to bribe a guard. They are making their way north, but have to be very careful. Josh has been in my thoughts so much. I relive that first kiss, over and over.

5 October 1863

A distant cousin has come to stay with us. Amelia is Cora's age, and has just seen her mother die of consumption. Her father is serving with the Union troops, and has not been heard from these several months. I fixed a cot for myself in the sewing room, so Amelia and Cora can share the small attic alcove. They make a cute pair; Amelia is tall and thin, whereas Cora is short like Mother. Mother says Amelia may become a permanent member of our family. Since Father is helping some families who have husbands and sons away, he does not have time to teach school this year. Rachel and I decided we would have some lessons of reading and arithmetic at our house, for a few children. The three young Baker children, the Johnston's two and the Marshall boys will join our Tommy and Cora. The twins, Henry and Grace, will also sit with us, however he is rather wiggly.

25 December 1863

We have had no word from our men. Mason's mother died a week ago from a lung infection. Leticia helped Rachel care for her in between Mother's visits. It's so sad that Mason doesn't even know. The weather is so cold with ice covering everything, that some of the tree limbs have cracked off or split. Father and Tommy spend most of the days tending to the livestock and chopping firewood. We had to bring the hens into the house after four froze yesterday. I unraveled an old sweater to knit Father and Mother each a pair of mittens for Christmas. Were it not for the twins, I believe we would have ignored the holiday altogether. I wonder if Josh is warm. Is he safe? Is he hungry?

23 February 1864

It seems that the only news to write about is bad news. We got word that Amelia's father was killed in a battle in Virginia. She cried and cried for days, and we all understood. I cannot even think about losing Father. Henry had a bad ear infection, which has affected the hearing in his right ear. Mother treated the infection with her remedy of warm onion juice, but it seems that the illness had to run its course. Little Grace sat by her twin's bedside, and they played with his tin soldier set when he felt well enough.

14 May 1864

Heavy spring rains flooded our fields, and took the seeds with it. Father was able to buy more seed, but many farmers are so poor now, they have no way to get another crop in the ground. Mr. Baker has declared he is ruined, so his family is packing up. Mrs. Baker begged him to stay in Bellville, but he is determined to move them to Louisiana. I pray Josh returns soon. I told Rachel that I love Josh. She laughed and said she had known for a long time. Rachel confided to me that the doctor's son has been walking her home from church. We haven't attended church in many months because Father says he thinks the preacher is sympathetic to the Confederate cause.

15 June 1864

I am eighteen years old today, but there is no time for celebration. Some of our livestock was stolen a few nights ago, and the small shed was burned to the ground. Tommy was burned on his face and back, while rescuing Father's horse. Mother has used all of her nursing skills to relieve his pain, and he seems to rest more comfortably today. I am so sick of this war! I long for the quiet, safe days when I was a child.

28 June 1864

Wonderful news…Tommy is much improved. Mother does not believe his face will have long lasting scars. Amelia is a great help to Mother in the kitchen, since she likes to cook more than I do. This summer I often spend evenings walking through our fields, sometimes ending up among the boulders on the mound. Old timers in the county say Indians used this place perhaps hundreds of years ago. We have uncovered stone tools and fragments of pottery among the rocks, and sometimes I feel like the place is magical. Anyway, that is what I tell myself. I try to imagine Josh alongside me, waiting for the stars to show themselves. Rachel and I have not ridden our horses very much this year, probably because I feel guilty when I am happy and carefree.

11 October 1864

Mister Brown showed us a letter he received from a farmer in Arkansas, who has allowed Mason and Josh to take refuge in his barn for several weeks. It is too dangerous for them to move about at this time, but if there is a chance, he will get them to Bellville. Leticia is beside herself, thinking that she will see Mason soon. Father says it is unfortunate we do not know where Josh's family is to tell them the news. I do not care about anyone in that family except Mrs. Baker and Josh, of course. Father and his friends believe the war will end soon. Gramps says he is so glad Missouri did not secede from the Union, since the south will be sorely punished for this devastating war.

21 February 1865

There is such turmoil in Bellville. Our once quiet and pleasant town is now frightening. Merchants are charging outrageous prices for simple foods and supplies. Strangers have moved into some of the farms and homes vacated by destitute families. Rachel's beau was killed on Christmas Day in Mississippi. He had only joined up in October. She says she'll never find anyone else to love. My own love is still missing with Mason. They left the farmer's hiding place in Arkansas, and we assume they are still making their way to Bellville. I feel so old, and worn down with worry. Mother is a rock of strength, but I can tell she is weary. Leticia moves quietly through the house, preoccupied with Mason's whereabouts. Cora and Amelia have each other's company, and that is good. Tommy has become a man out of necessity, since Father depends on his help with all the farm work. Henry and Grace are able to take on a few chores now.

23 March 1865

The news is that the south is crumbling and Rebel soldiers are deserting by the thousands. This war must end soon. Our root cellars are almost empty, but only because my parents are always helping out folks who have nothing to eat. There are a few cabbages and turnips left, as well as some onions and dried peas. The last of our yams were eaten two weeks ago, and unfortunately the smokehouse contains one lonely rasher of bacon. The chickens still supply us with eggs, and an occasional dinner. The woods do not seem to have much game this year. There is not an ounce of flour to be had at any price in the county, so Mother grinds corn for all our breads. Corn meal mush, cooled, sliced and fried, drizzled with honey, is the usual morning meal. Thank goodness we do have the honey!

12 April 1865
The war is over!!! Lee surrendered to Grant on the seventh of this month. We pray that Mason and Josh are able to make their way home without having to hide along the way. Mother killed three chickens to fix for a celebration, inviting Rachel and Mr. Brown. Granny used the last of their sugar and flour to make a spice cake. I rode my horse into town to invite the new pastor and his wife. For myself and Leticia, it is hard to celebrate without Mason and Josh here. Cora is so sweet, hugging me and saying she is sure our sweethearts will be home soon.

17 April 1865
This is a black day. President Lincoln has been murdered.

29 April 1865
Lincoln's murderer was found and killed. His death will not bring President Lincoln back, but somehow I feel a measure of justice has been handed down.

1 May 1865
Father has cautioned us all to watch out for soldiers making their way home. They will be hungry and inclined to steal what they need.

Mother says any soldier, north or south, who appears at the kitchen door, will be given a plate of food. I cannot sleep for wondering where Josh is. Perhaps he and Mason are nearing Bellville right now, having been fed by a nice lady like Mother.

13 August 1865

Josh has been here over two months. He is very sick, both in body and mind. Josh and Mason suffered from scurvy while in prison camp and after their escape. They had neither hot food nor enough to eat for a long time. Leticia sobbed all night after spending the first afternoon with Mason. Since Josh's family is gone he is staying with us, so Mother and I can nurse him. Both men had open sores on their legs and have lost some teeth. We had to coax Josh to eat. In the beginning, he would sob when food was placed on the table, saying over and over that the men were so hungry. It was as if he felt guilty, suddenly having so much food on his plate. I had dreamed of a different kind of reunion when he returned. Leticia says Mason's health is steadily improving, and he has told her more about their time in the prison camps. They witnessed terribly cruel treatment, and watched friends starve to death or die of disease and untreated injuries.

15 October 1865

Leticia and Mason plan to marry in December. He is just so happy to be home and safe, and is ready to make a life for Leticia and him. I wish I could say the same for Josh. He is gradually improving physically, but his nerves are broken. Josh sits and stares across the meadow for hours in the daytime; at night he sleeps fitfully, having nightmares usually accompanied by yelling for his fellow prisoners. Sometimes Father wakes Josh, and they talk awhile. I am worried that my love is not enough to cure him, but I am going to try. We are still suffering from severe shortages in some goods, but Father says a boot maker has moved to Bellville. The whole family will have new shoes and boots before Christmas! The boot maker is a light skinned son of a mulatto couple who came with him from Tennessee. Another new person in town is a school teacher from Jefferson City. Father is elated that our family can hand that job over to someone else, since our farm has grown so large. He has volunteered to help build a real school next to the Methodist church.

11 December 1865

Missouri Confederate soldiers and sympathizers are finding these times very hard. Life will never be the same for anyone, especially families who lost loved ones, like us. Yesterday was unseasonably mild, so I begged Josh to ride with me to Clinton to purchase a special wedding present for Leticia and Mason. He is slowly becoming interested in life going on around him, and the ride did him a world of good. Being impractical, we chose a framed painting of a small village nestled on the banks of the Mississippi River. It looks so peaceful and reminds me of life before the war.

25 December 1865

Leticia and Mason were married on the twenty first. Mr. Brown gave them fifty acres of his land, but they will live with him and Rachel until their own house is built. Josh is still so quiet, but he likes to help Father and Tommy with chores. I believe he wants to be exhausted by the day's end, so he can fall asleep easier. I actually heard him laugh for the first time since coming home, when Tommy slipped and landed in a foul barnyard pile. I ran into the house to tell Mother, and we both cried. When I went to bed last night, I found a note on my pillow from Josh. He does love me!! He asks me to be patient, and I can do that.

17 January 1866

Rachel says she saw a new young man at church last week, and was told that Robert Colley is a new attorney from St. Louis, practicing with old Mr. Reed. The next day when she took a basket of preserves to widow Carter, she discovered that Robert was lodging in that same house. He was invited to join the two women for coffee which resulted in quite an interesting afternoon. Robert lost an arm at Gettysburg, fighting the Rebels, yet Rachel says he has adjusted well. I am so happy she once again welcomes a male friend. Josh and I move as in a strange dance, not quite touching, but always aware of each other. The nightmares are becoming fewer, he says, but for the last month he has bunked in the barn, so if he yells out it will no longer wake the family.

31 January 1866

Gramps and Granny Lee helped us plan a surprise party for Father and Mother to celebrate twenty-five years of marriage. Mother's black hair is showing a little gray now, and Father laughs that he is getting thin on top, but both of them remain young at heart. Mr. Brown came with Leticia and Mason and brought his fiddle. Rachel brought Robert Colley, and later I confided to her that he seems very intelligent and is handsome too. Henry and Grace danced a reel with the family, surprising us all that they knew how. Our shy Tommy avoided dancing, but Mother was pleased to hear him tell Mr. Brown that he wants to learn to play the fiddle. Cora and Amelia helped Granny fill the table with the foods secretly prepared in Granny's kitchen. Cora asked Josh to be her partner when Mr. Brown started playing *Put Your Little Foot*. He had been an onlooker until then, but graciously accepted. Cora giggled and curtsied when the dance ended. Josh's eyes searched the room, and I brazenly stepped forward to take his hand. Mr. Brown took the cue and played *Annie Laurie*. The room was still, except for Josh and me, and I had the feeling that we were alone, waltzing around and around. It was magic. The evening ended at two o'clock in the morning. I walked with Josh to the barn, and would have stayed if Mother hadn't called from the porch that we all needed to get to bed. But I couldn't sleep, savoring the kiss Josh quickly gave me in the shadows.

8 February 1866

It is snowing and blowing so hard. Father, Tommy and Josh gathered the livestock into the barn when they saw heavy clouds overtaking the hills yesterday. All we can do is stay indoors, and keep busy with little chores. Today Father is working in the barn on a cupboard Mother wants for the parlor. Last week, Josh rode over to the house where his parents had lived, and asked the new owners if any of his books were left behind. The Joneses are a kind old couple, who have a crippled son living with them. Not only did they have Josh's books, but the young man loaned us some of his own. I have begun reading aloud *Robinson Crusoe*, and the whole family says these evenings are the best part of their days.

1 March 1866

Oh, I cannot contain my happiness! Josh asked Father for my hand in marriage. Mother told me they were not surprised at all. We will marry in May!

13 April 1866

We buried Gramps today. Granny found him dead in his chair when she came in from gathering eggs. Father says he didn't suffer, and that is a blessing. Cora and Amelia will stay with Granny for now, and our men will take care of the chores. It is a very sad time for us, as Gramps was a perfectly sweet grandfather, who only thought of others. Father will miss him terribly.

3 May 1866

Josh and I will marry tomorrow, and he seems as happy as I am. We have so many plans for the future, and are anxious to start a family. Mother and Leticia helped me sew some new clothes, and many neighbors have given us crockery and linens for our future home. We will stay in Granny Lee's house and farm the land, until she decides what to do. Leticia is going to have a baby! She has told only Mother and me, and Mason of course. It will come toward the end of October.

23 August 1869

It has been over three years since I last wrote; our lives have sped along, with many happy and some sad events. Leticia has two little boys, and. we have been blessed with a boy now two years old and a new baby girl. My son's name is Mitchell, after Mother's maiden name, and my daughter is Irene, after Josh's mother. Tragically, we lost my little sister, Grace, when her appendix ruptured a year ago. I worried so about Mother, but she mourned privately, and tended to her family as usual. We all miss Grace's sweet personality and big heart. We still live in Granny's house since she transferred ownership of her farm to Josh and me, except for 60 acres near the river which she deeded to Tommy. During the war Granny kept hidden a sterling silver tea service, and twelve place settings of silverware, which she divided between Leticia and Cora. This silver has been passed down through her family, and brought to the America's from England about one hundred years ago. Granny will give Henry five hundred dollars when he turns 18. Amelia will be given a dowry of fifty dollars. Granny says she feels better about giving her belongings away while she is alive, instead of having a will read after she dies. Josh and I are very happy and have a bundle of plans for improving the farm. Cora and Amelia have both just celebrated their eighteenth birthdays. Amelia has a beau and Cora is studying to be a teacher. Tommy still farms with Father and plays the fiddle for any and every occasion. Henry wants to be in the circus, ha, ha; however, in the meantime he helps Father when he is not in school. Rachel and Robert married a year ago, and live in a fine house in town.

25 December 1869
Our Christmas dinner table was surrounded with all of our family, and many friends. My cup runneth over.

5 May 5 1870
I am living a nightmare. It began when Mother asked Leticia, Cora and me to come to the house while our men were away. She told us a shocking secret she felt no one else except Father knew, or so she thought, until a person in town came to her speaking of it. Mother told Father about this before they married, but we will not tell Josh or Mason. Keeping something so important from my dear husband goes against the kind of marriage we have built, but it must be. I cannot write the details, but Mother feels it is best to leave Bellville. Leticia knows Mason will never move, so she will take her chances that the secret will not circulate after most of us move away. Father, in his usual way of doing what has to be done, is going to tell friends that he wants to move west while he is young enough to start over. He surprised even Mother by suggesting we join his cousins in Colorado, ranching or mining. I just hope that Josh will voluntarily suggest we join my family, so I won't have to be the one insisting that we follow them.

Rosalie wondered just who approached Susan's mother with knowledge of something that she had kept secret for so long. Perhaps Martha's father was a swindler or felon.

7 May 1870

Mason will take care of selling our two farms. He is very confused that Father never mentioned a desire to see the west, but he is adamant that they will stay in Bellville. His father passed away last winter and left the remaining land to them. Granny declares she is too old for such a journey, so she will stay with Leticia's family. Mother is so shaken that the family will be split up. My sweet Josh was so worried I would not want to move, and relief flooded his face when I said I would go anywhere with him. He told me that he had dreamed of going west one day but had not thought it was possible since my family was so established in Missouri. Father quietly reminded his daughters not to mention to Granny the true reason for leaving. She and Mother have had the best friendship all these years, but Granny might not understand why Mother and Father kept such a secret from her. Father is troubled by Mother's frantic packing and sleepless nights. We plan to leave in three weeks, driving three wagons. I cannot give into the devastation I feel, including the reason for leaving my home, Leticia, Granny and Rachel. Mother moves nervously about the house as if someone is going to burst in the door. Sometimes she just sits and watches the children play, tears filling her eyes. I just don't know what to do for her.

10 May 1870

Amelia suddenly packed her things and left. She said she knew of a job in Clinton, and wanted Cora to come with her. Cora told me she must move with us, or Mother might think she resents this new revelation. All three of us are quite resolved about it, I suppose, because of Father's acceptance all these years. Amelia is angry at our sudden packing up to move over eight hundred miles west. Not being privy to our secret, she accused Mother of not caring enough about her happiness. Father had planned to give Amelia money to tide her over awhile, but when he heard what she said to Mother, he just turned away when she walked out the door. Leticia says she will keep her eye on Amelia, and offer her a room in their home. Mother blames herself for Amelia's reaction, choosing to keep her ignorant of the real facts. Cora is the one who feels the real loss. Tommy told Father that he wants to stay in Bellville. He offered to help us make the journey to Colorado, but Father said we can manage if I drive one of the wagons. I know this was a difficult decision for Tommy, but he has always been so close to Leticia and Mason. A few weeks ago we were so carefree, just worrying about baby Irene's teething and getting new shoes for Mitch. Leticia comes over every day to help us pack crates and trunks with clothes, preserved food, tools and as much of our dishes and cookware as possible. Mother and I hope to take as much furniture as the wagons can carry. Father gave some of our livestock to Mason, and sold some to help buy oxen to pull the wagons to Colorado. Each of the wagons will have a saddle horse tied onto the tailgate. Mother insists on taking a crate of chickens which I am sure we will appreciate along the way. Henry will follow the wagons, driving a dozen head of cattle. Rachel doesn't understand our decision to move away. We both had dreamed of watching our children grow up together. I am sad I will not be here when her first baby is born in three months, but we promise each other we will write.

24 May 1870
The wagons are packed, and I wish I could say Mother and I are excited to point the teams towards Colorado. There have been so

many tears in the last week, and I cannot stand one more person saying how much we will be missed. I overheard Father quietly saying to Mother, "Martha, I could never find a more perfect wife and mother of my children." He keeps assuring her that this move will be good for the family in the end. Dearest Josh declares this move an adventure, with our family joining so many others helping to settle the far west. Two of Father's cousins on Granny's side of the family trekked to Colorado when gold was discovered at Pike's Peak, but last year Luke wrote that he and cousin Matthew are working for a Mr. Cassidy, refining petroleum discovered near Canon City. Josh and Father will find work, and when the farms here are sold, we plan to buy new land to farm or ranch, and get back to what is familiar. I just want a good, secure life for my children. Speaking of children, I believe I am carrying a child again. Josh does not know yet, and since Irene is still nursing, I am shocked to be with child so soon.

6 June 1870
Today is Mitchell's birthday! His favorite food is hotcakes, so that will be his birthday supper, with lots of honey. Father says Independence, Missouri is just a few days distant.

28 June 1870
We finally left Independence, where wagons gather to join trains heading west, and are slowly making our way across Kansas. Our three wagons are traveling with twenty-two others, following the old Santa Fe Trail. Father says that about half of the wagons, including ours, will separate from the train in western Kansas to stay pointed west for Pueblo, Colorado. From there Canon City is about 3 more days into the mountains. It is nicer out on the prairie, instead of being jostled about in Independence. While we were waiting to depart, I wrote Leticia a long letter to share with the family in Bellville. I so

wish they were with us. Mother is so lost and sad that she isn't much company as she sits on the wagon seat beside me. Cora has proven to be indispensable in caring for Mitch and Irene while I am driving the team. I am so tired at the end of each day, after pulling and jerking on the reins, Mother usually takes over cooking over the campfire that Father quickly arranges. My back hurts so by mid-afternoon, from the bouncing and swaying, I sometimes have Henry drive for a little while. He does very well, and I believe he will be able to take over in a week or two since one of our new friends has offered to bunch our herd with his own, freeing Henry from trailing cattle.

12 July 1870
We halted at the settlement of Council Grove, which gave the families a chance to buy what they forgot to pack. In my case, it was knitting needles. I am trying to keep my condition a secret awhile longer otherwise Josh will not want me to work so hard. Other than being a little sick late in the mornings, I feel fine. Mother may suspect, but she says nothing. I am worried about her being so withdrawn; she remarks very little of our surroundings unless I prod her, and remains aloof to the children's needs. Today the men spied some bison in a far off valley, and a hunting party was dispatched. Josh joined them and returned with a triumphant smile and meat for every family.

15 July 1870
A few nights ago Mr. Lunsford, the wagon master, asked Mother if she could help a young woman with the birth of her first child. It was a breech birth, but Mother was able to deliver the baby safely after a long night. The next day Josh, Father and I noticed a change in Mother's mood. She was tired but played with the children all morning. At the noon rest, I talked her into taking a little nap. When

we stopped for the night, she killed one of her chickens and put the pieces on to simmer over the campfire. After checking on the new mother and baby, Mother added dumplings to the cooked meat and broth. Father complimented Mother on the meal as he cut into a large skillet of cornbread, and Josh opened a jar of wild plum preserves to spoon over the crispy topped, spongy slices. Henry hugged Mother as if she had been away.

22 July 1870

Henry has taken over driving the wagon for me every morning after he helps get the cattle herd rounded up and started on the trail. I can help Cora with the children now, so she has some free time during the day. Mother enjoys riding along with Father in their wagon, or helping ill travelers.

29 July 1870

Our oxen are suffering from too little grass, and sparse water. The sun makes the air so hot; even shade offers little relief. Children are fussy, especially the younger ones who have to be kept in the wagons all day. A young woman, who rides horseback much of the time, takes Mitchell on short rides, which delight our big boy to no end. Mother has now become someone the wagon train depends on for council involving the health and well being of women and children. Many a mother has thanked her for demanding the wagon train halt for an occasional day of washing clothes, and resting bodies. I can understand her need to feel helpful. A preacher traveling to Santa Fe holds Sunday services. During the first few weeks on the trail we halted for the day, but now, right after services the oxen are yoked and the wagons roll. Irene and Mitch have been healthy so far, but we have heard some wagon trains experience cholera epidemics. We have seen a few savages that Mr. Lunsford identified as Osage and Kiowa—they are pitifully ragged and dirty. Our men watch the livestock closely, to prevent any stealing. Father argued with Mr. Lunsford that we should give them some food, but our wagon master said if we do, they will follow us all the way across Kansas. Officially we don't give the savages anything, but I watched Father hand one old man a bulging sack, motioning him quickly on his way.

3 August 1870

Josh and a few other men rode out to find some game, and returned with four antelope. Tonight there was meat, not beans, in every pot or spit over a campfire. The trail we follow has been used by hundreds, if not thousands, of wagons. The dust is deep and powdery, stirred into clouds that at times obscure the wagon in front of ours. Mother wipes the children's faces several times a day, but all of us suffer from irritated eyes and throats. Before any of us crawl onto the pallets at night, the bed covers have to be shaken free of the grit and grime.

16 August 1870

We reached the Great Bend on the Arkansas River few days ago and purchased some feed for the horses at a small trading post. Today we approach Fort Larned, where a few wagons will have parts repaired by the fort's blacksmith. In the last week we passed several small encampments of Indians and saw one family butchering a bison. Mr. Lunsford told us that in two or three years, the railroad will reach this far across Kansas. Perhaps when I return to Bellville to see Leticia, I can take the train all the way from Colorado to Missouri! I have written a few short letters to the folks back in Bellville. Father also asked me to write his cousins in Canon City, advising them of our progress. Our wagon master tells us this stop is the last place where we can post letters, until we reach Pueblo. Our boy Mitch fell from the back of the wagon and got a bad bump on his head. Cora was changing Irene's clothes when Mitch declared he wanted to ride with Paw-Paw, and out he tumbled. I was just thankful he wasn't run over by the team following us. Josh saw him fall onto the dusty trail, and was able to pull up. Father and Mother are more light-hearted lately, and each day they discuss the possibilities in Colorado. I have faith we also will be happy there. Somehow I intend to see Leticia, Rachel and Tommy again before too many years pass.

2 September 1870

We now travel with fewer wagons since several turned off for Santa Fe. We continue westward with Father as our guide, using the map provided by Mr. Lunsford. When we get to Canon City, I do not want to cross any more rivers, ever! Irene had a fever last night and I was frantic because I just knew she had contracted cholera. Mother sat with me all night, bathing Irene's little body. This morning my darling awoke cool to the touch and hungry. Josh has been so worried about accidents and illness on the trail. Since he believes it was his idea to go west with Father, he would blame himself if anything happened. I know the truth; it would be Mother blaming herself. All of my family now know about our new baby coming around Christmas, and Josh is very happy. Henry says I should have a boy and name it after him.

4 September 1870

The thick trail dust has now become wet, sticky, mud after a terrific thunder storm last night. We had never witnessed the intensity of such rain, whipping in solid sheets upon the wagons and our poor livestock. Several wagons have torn canvases which have to be mended, and some cattle have wandered off. Our shoes build up with four-inch soles of mud when we make our way around the camp. Oh, I am so weary of dirt and wind.

14 September 1870
Mother managed to get Father to agree to a full day's rest to celebrate our crossing into Colorado Territory. I do not know how much rest anyone got since the women washed clothes in the river, and spread them to dry on the surrounding brush. The men worked on harnesses and crooned to their animals. Everyone who wanted to bathe took advantage of a leisurely soak in the slow moving river, and some who did not, needed to! Having clean hair always makes me feel like a woman again. Mitch and Irene splashed in the warm shallows until their fingers were wrinkled. On this journey, Cora has made friends with a young lady and her brother who are traveling to Pueblo to join their father. The three of them packed a picnic lunch and could be seen across a small tributary that joins the Arkansas River. I couldn't blame them for wanting to talk and laugh without being interrupted by others. After sunset they joined us around a large campfire, and I suddenly felt very matronly. Josh must have read my mind; he pulled me close to him and whispered that he hoped I am happy, because he is. We have been talking about names for the baby. Josh hopes for a boy who will be named James Henry.

20 September 1870
Today we passed the ruins of an old trading post built three decades ago by the Bent brothers. The country here is so barren and lonesome. The days are still very warm, but nights are almost too cool. The baby clothes I have made almost fill the small hamper. Mother is piecing a baby quilt like she did for Irene and Mitch. It takes a real effort to remain patient with the children, as they are bored and irritable with the dust bothering them all day.

29 September 1870

Pueblo at last! We can see Pike's Peak towering over the plains. The west is certainly a mysterious place. It feels as old as the ages, and is so vast that my vision rebels while trying to take in the panoramic spectacle. Father insists we should have a party to celebrate the end of a long journey. He bought some large fish—trout I believe—that we baked in the campfire coals. Mother, Cora and I will stay here with the wagons and children, while Father and Josh travel by horseback to Canon City to find the cousins.

Rosalie put the diary down and rubbed her eyes. Susan had become quite real to her, and she was glad the young woman seemed happy with the thought of a new life in Colorado. Josh was satisfied with the move, so the secret could stay buried in Missouri—but did it?

30 September 1870

Cora and I are busily mending tattered clothes, patching the many holes worn through elbows and knees. Much to my surprise, the small mercantile in the settlement stocks a variety of fabric, so I purchased enough for some new shirts, blouses, underwear, and skirts we will sew over the winter. Before we leave Pueblo, the whole family will get new shoes, and all of the men and boys need new pants too. Cora visited her friends, Michael and Regina Pope, at their home this afternoon and returned full of chatter and twinkling eyes.

1 October 1870

I took the children to Mr. Scott's shop, where they were fitted with sturdy leather shoes. Mrs. Scott took Cora's and my foot measurements and promised that our shoes will be ready within four days. Knowing that in three months I will have my baby far from a town, I sought a doctor for an examination. Dr. Cole says the baby's heartbeat is strong, and I should get more rest. He also says there is a midwife in Canon City, in addition to his visits every two weeks. Last night a fire destroyed a makeshift hotel, but no one was killed. I am so glad we decided to stay in our own wagons at the edge of town. At night we hear gunfire nearby, mostly on the street where the saloons are located. Mother is afraid something is going to happen to one of the children. Henry is too curious about the men roaming through town wearing gun belts. Irene has a cough. I hope the men find the cousins and come back soon.

5 October 1870

Irene has been so sick! One whole night I sat up rocking her. The doctor came and confirmed she had the croup, so I built a little tent over her, and steamed the enclosure with the tea kettle. Irene is still coughing, but Mother says she is over the worst, thank god. Cora picked up our new shoes from Mr. Scott, four dollars. Father and Josh should be returning soon. Michael Pope brought our family a beef stew prepared by their cook, and fetched Cora to join his family at a musical gathering. He was kind enough to invite the whole family, but Mother and I want to stay close to our camp, in case the men show up. We scurried around inside the wagon, fixing Cora's hair and retrieving her best dress from a trunk we had not opened since leaving Missouri. She looked quite fetching in her blue shirtwaist, bonnet, and new shoes. Cora's dark hair sets off her fine features and pale complexion.

6 October 1870

There is still no sign of Josh or Father and we all are very worried. Last night Henry disappeared after supper, and did not return until after midnight. I was furious that he had upset Mother so much. When he told us what he had been doing, we had to soften our scolding.

Henry had been working, delivering buckets of beer, shuttling from one of the saloons to the hotels and gambling tents. He worked for tips and when he proudly handed Mother the six dollars, she said half of it was his to keep. Henry would have been disappointed if Mother had refused it all. Mitch took a tumble this afternoon, and chipped one of his front teeth. This evening I let out the waistbands of two skirts.

8 October 1870

Father and Josh are back! When they arrived in Canon City, they found that the Carter families recently moved a few miles away to a gold claim. It took two more days to locate them, but now Josh has a list of supplies to buy for the claim. Father seems awfully tired, so I convinced Josh we should stay here another day before heading up into the craggy mountains. Michael and Regina came to say good-by although I have a feeling we will see Michael again before long.

20 October 1870

Once we arrived at the mine, the men wasted no time in cutting logs for our cabin. With help from our extended family, we were able to move out of the wagons into the small cabin just yesterday. It feels so good to have four walls and a roof over our heads. The gaps between the logs have to be chinked, which is left to the women while the men get back to mining. Our little family settlement is about fifteen miles from Canon City, with mines strung along the trails. Most of the cabins have only men occupants; the few women we saw seemed hungry for female conversation. Luke and Matthew's wives, Millie and Roberta, are such sweet mothers to their own broods, and mine too. I feel sleepy so much of the time, but Millie says it takes awhile to get accustomed to this altitude. Irene is now weaned, in preparation for the new baby.

21 November 1870

All we see is white: up the mountain, down the mountain, covering the trees and cabins. The weather is so cold the branches of trees crack, sounding like a gunshot in the forest. The men are still able to work in the mine for now, and with two more men working, Josh says they are making fast progress sinking the shaft. Josh and Father have bought shares of the mine, and they hope to hit a vein soon, like some folks on a neighboring claim. The children are already tired of being cooped up inside; it is going to be a long winter. There is no mid-wife in this area, and the doctor does not come this far up the mountain. However, Millie will assist Mother when my baby comes. It is such a relief to have the families around us.

11 February 1871

Our little boy, James Henry, is now six weeks old. He was born robust and energetic, which pleases his father to no end! Mitchell and Irene think their little brother is very funny. The cabin is terribly cramped with all of us and a new baby. Michael Pope came in a sled to fetch Cora for a two week stay in Pueblo with Regina. Cora talked to me about taking a teaching position, since teachers are badly needed everywhere. Although she is not fully trained, both the Pueblo and Canon City schools will hire her. The snow is still very deep in our mountains. Millie's little girl was sick with a fever, but I believe she is better today.

4 July 1871

The men took the day off from the mine to join the Canon City community in celebrating Independence Day. A year ago we were making our way across Kansas. Cora will teach school in Pueblo this fall; Regina's father has generously invited her to live in their home, which helped persuade Mother and Father she would be safe in the settlement. Our mine has proven to have a modest vein of gold, but Father was not satisfied in this business, and has sold his share back to Luke and his brother. Father's farm in Missouri has been sold, so he bought land near Pueblo and has returned to farming and ranching. Josh intends to keep mining here for the time being, but I wish we lived nearer a real town. Henry will be able to attend school where Father relocated the family. In another two years Mitchell will be old enough for school, so I hope we have moved by then. Irene and James are healthy as can be. I miss having Mother with me every day.

8 July 1871
Josh went to Canon City for supplies right after Independence Day, and found a letter from Mother had just arrived. The sad news is that Granny Lee has passed away. Of course Mother regrets that she wasn't with Granny at the end. A letter from Leticia followed, full of news, with more details of Granny. The stroke was quick so she didn't suffer, and that is a relief. Granny and Gramps now lay side by side in the family cemetery on the land she gave to Tommy. He has worked this last year at a saw mill, earning enough to begin construction on a small house. Leticia has not been able to locate Amelia to tell her about Granny. She says that it is very quiet in Bellville. I think this means there is no talk about the thing we must keep secret. Mason's farm is doing very well, with large grain harvests, colts, calves and lambs. A new baby was born to them two months ago, Mason James whom they call M.J.

28 October 1871
Another winter on the mountain is facing us! It is lonesome without Mother and Father, but at least we can see them in the spring.

Our mine is playing out. Luke and Mathew will be moving their families to Canon City in the spring, and I pray Josh will be ready to give up this endeavor. We have saved a good amount of money, and our farm in Missouri sold a few weeks ago. Cora enjoys her teaching position, and she has become quite a city girl. I have sorely missed her company.

26 December 1871
Our Christmas was spent without Mother, Father, and Henry for the first time in my life. Since Cora is able to see Mother and Father occasionally, she chose to spend Christmas with us. Michael brought her up the mountain, and they both stayed two wonderful days. Our family and the cousins celebrated Christmas with good food and games. There was a lot of squealing and laughing when children opened presents. I do dread when the cousins leave, especially Millie.

19 December 1872
This year has gone by without time for daily notes on our lives, but as Christmas comes around again, I must record the events of most importance. I have hardly had time to sleep, much less write. Last spring Luke and Matthew left the mountain and we followed in June. Josh thought he would like working in Canon City, but we only stayed there a month. He found a ranch for sale in the foothills, so we moved there in August. Our money made it possible to build a nice four room house, and also buy a number of longhorns and horses. Josh will try growing different grains to find the one that does the best on this land. We welcomed a new daughter, Elizabeth, to the family in October, so I have had four children in five years. Josh seems to be satisfied with his life and proud of the children. Mother and Father are within a day's ride which makes me very happy. Henry

excels at school, claiming he wants to be a mining engineer. Rachel's husband Robert handled the transfer of money Granny left for Henry, which will cover most of his expenses at college. Cora and Michael were married in Pueblo two months ago in a wedding she had always dreamed about. Cora has assimilated into the social life of a well to do family. I feel dowdy next to her in my home sewn clothes, but Cora is not a bit pretentious.

11 April 1873

The purple foothills are my favorite sunset view, and the children love it too. Sometimes we can get Josh to accompany us on a ride to a nearby hill across the meadow, for a better view of the mountains to the west. Without a doubt, the last several months have been our best since leaving Bellville. The ranch is going to be a success, I just know, and a place where the children will grow up secure, with family nearby. Mitch and Irene have playmates on neighboring ranches, and will attend school with them soon. James Henry and Lizzie are too young to appreciate our new life in the Rockies' Front Range, but I know they will love it as much as the rest of us.

4 January 1874

Almost a year has passed since I last wrote, and although I feel that I should pick up pen again, it is with a heavy heart. Josh is dissatisfied here, which means we must move again. He says he is tired of the cold winters and deep snow. We have lost much of our money to a scheme Josh bought into that promised a large return; after bleeding us dry, the broker disappeared. I have no idea where Josh will have us go, but as far as I am concerned, separating us from my family will not do. He recently expressed regret that we left Missouri, which made my heart freeze. Josh has lately become quiet and withdrawn. I cannot believe he has changed so much, and I believe that I have too. Father and Mother have seen this change in Josh and worry about us. The bright spots in my own life are my children.

20 February 1874

Josh came home from Pueblo this afternoon, announcing he had sold the ranch, and we are moving back to Bellville! As much as I want to see Leticia and Tommy, it is impossible to return without risking a scandal. I am so upset I told Josh I am taking the children to Mother's for a few days.

15 March 1874

Our life has become a silent struggle for civility. To prevent Josh from taking us back to Bellville, where there is always the chance someone will come forward to expose us, I told him the guarded secret. His reaction was not at all what I expected; in fact, I was terrified of him. Later he claimed he was most upset that I kept a secret from him, not by the actual thing itself. I don't believe him since he seemed horrified when I spoke the words. He has tried to make it up to the children, who were so frightened when they walked in on his rage. We loaded as much as possible into one wagon pulled by two mules and struck out for Father's ranch. I had no idea where we would go from there, but then Josh revealed that he wants to go to Texas. I begged and cried, Father became angry, and Mother berated him; Josh would not be swayed. I am so afraid for our family. Stories about the wilderness in Texas, with marauding Indians and outlaws, are familiar to us all. We tried to convince Josh to leave us here until he at least found a settlement that would suit us. He countered that Elizabeth and I could stay, but Mitch, Irene, and James Henry were going with him. Mother asked Josh for one more day, so she could celebrate all four of the grandchildren's birthdays. We adults bit our tongues as my darlings ate cake and opened impromptu presents. Four children and their two sullen parents climbed into the wagon and turned east. Two days southeast of Pueblo a blizzard caught us in a draw, where we had camped for the night. Our tent was almost completely buried with snow by the next morning. The children remained wrapped in quilts a whole day except when we would allow one at a time out to eat some cold meat and biscuits I had cooked the evening before the blizzard. Although the children thought it was a great game, we knew it could turn into a deadly situation if the blizzard continued very long. The next morning the skies were clear so we dug out. The poor mules had been turned out to find their own shelter or lee in the storm, but they hadn't gone far. Soon after leaving the camp we found an empty ramshackle cabin where we stayed two more days in relative comfort, waiting for some of the snow to melt. Josh barely addresses me directly; I know he hates being married to me now. I never imagined such total sadness, and my chest hurts as if a dagger had pierced my heart. Were it not for Mitchell, Irene, James Henry, and Elizabeth I would gladly leave, and he probably feels the same way.

28 March 1874

Last night we camped near some soldiers who invited Josh to their fire to exchange news. Some of the soldiers had been to Texas and recommended an area just south of the Red River as prime land. They also warned Josh that the shortest way to Texas, across the Llano Estacado or Staked Plains, was too dangerous because of Comanche attacks. We will have to travel east into Oklahoma, then turn south through Fort Sill to avoid trouble. After crossing the Red River into Texas, Josh will start looking for land. He is determined to not use our ranch money during the travels, so he hunts along the way, selling meat to the forts and railroad construction crews we come across.

27 April 1874

Our progress is slow with wagon repairs and illness. The Canadian River crossing was difficult since several wagons were already mired in quicksand. Teams were rigged to pull them out before we could cross. Josh spent the morning exploring along the banks to find a safer place to take the wagon across. For a little while I was proud of Josh's attention to our safety, almost forgetting the two of us were barely speaking. Irene's eyes had become very irritated, even though I often washed dust from them. We stopped in Fort Sill for a doctor to see her, and the treatment took about a week to cure the inflammation. I welcomed the rest, and enjoyed visiting with some of the soldiers' wives. Josh purchased a fine saddle horse, which the children promptly named Red. He is strong and gentle, perfect for our family. Josh's trip out with a hunting party for bison earned him four dollars. We spent most of it on sugar, flour, and shoes for Mitchell.

9 May 1874

I sewed new sunbonnets for myself and Irene, since her little face is getting brown as a nut. Thankfully Irene's eyes remain clear and bright. We heard of an Indian attack just after crossing the Red River. A remote ranch house was burned by a band of Comanche, who killed a man and took his wife captive. When we moved to Colorado, being in a wagon train gave us some measure of security; however, traveling alone I feel very exposed, and we are repeatedly warned against it. One thing Josh and I agree about is keeping the children close to the wagon as we make our way south through the tall grass and thickets which could easily hide the savages. Josh dozes a few hours in the daytime while I drive the team, since he keeps watch most all nights.

Rosalie reread the last entry and again wondered why Susan's husband put their family into such danger, traveling alone all the miles from Colorado into the wild Texas prairie. Susan had such a pleasant life and safe surroundings for her children before Josh decided on this journey through desolate Indian country.

31 May 1874

Game is plentiful and Josh has been able to shoot a good number of antelope, turkeys and deer. He sells the meat and hides in small settlements along the way. We have stopped at Cambridge in Clay County so I can clean and repack the wagon. Mitchell is so helpful, as he plays with the younger children while I am busy. Josh is repairing some harness, and a wheel needs a blacksmith's hand. Most of the inhabitants here are buffalo hunters, who curse until the air turns blue! The trading post's owner is an older man with a wife about my age. Marcella Bergen and I have spent several afternoons talking about our lives before the war, and becoming wives and mothers. Of course, we reveal only superficial facts of ourselves. I believe she has some secrets about her marriage, as I do. Josh has not come to me at night since we left Pueblo.

2 August 1874

Our route has twisted past small settlements, remote ranches, lush valleys, dry riverbeds, and snake infested cliffs. I have worried myself sleepless about the children's safety. Several times we camped in grassy valleys that seemed a good place to build a ranch. I don't understand why Josh is never satisfied with the land we cross. Upon reaching San Saba, where Josh says we will stay a week or two, he joined a hunting party to earn some hard cash for supplies. Our vagabond existence is no longer a lark for the children; I believe they yearn for a roof as much as I. I am so weary of trying to keep the children clean and fed, with only campfires for preparing meals. Little Lizzie frets much of the time, having to stay in the wagon all day. My arms ache so much just from holding her or taking a turn at driving the mules.

12 August 1874

Our wagon has turned back for Cambridge. I would have liked living in San Saba; however, Josh says sheep are the prevailing ranch stock, and he does not want a sheep ranch.

5 October 1874

Josh rented a small house for us in Cambridge, where the children and I are living while he expands his search for land. A surveyor told him about a place he just saw that is west of the Wichita River falls. They left this morning and Josh said he might be gone two or three weeks. To live in a real house again is wonderful! Cooking on a real stove, pumping water a few steps from the kitchen, and being able to lock the doors mean so much. Mitchell is my little man while his pa is gone. He is very good at entertaining James Henry while I wash and clean. Irene has schooled Lizzie in the correct way to play house, which they do for hours. I am so lucky to have such sweet children. The whole family needs new clothing, so I spent six dollars for goods to sew shirts and dresses for the children while I have the time. Josh's shirts are full of patches and my skirts are threadbare. Marcella Bergen came by today, and I look forward to many afternoon visits with her. She is so pretty, and I just wonder why she married a gruff, old man.

Marcella's little boy suffered from a high fever when he was a baby, and he cannot talk or play like other three year old children. I am so thankful my boys and girls are healthy.

15 October 1874

Lizzie has been very sick and feverish. The doctor here is old and drunk most of the time, but he gave Lizzie some foul tasting medicine which helped the fever go down. James Henry was stung by several wasps while climbing a tree. We haven't seen or heard from Josh. Mitchell is attending the one room school next to the Methodist Church, and he told me that they read easy books so I guess all my time teaching the children is worth it. I have been teaching Irene her letters and numbers.

25 December 1874

Josh returned in mid-October with stories of lush, rolling hills and head-high grass, all located on Beaver Creek about fifty miles west of Cambridge. He filed on three hundred and twenty acres and paid for a survey to be done in the spring. Josh spent twenty-five dollars on lumber from a mill northwest of Beaver Creek, and he hired a teamster to haul it to the new site. He plans to spend the winter building a two room cabin, digging a cellar, and cutting poles for a corral. Josh hired a young man to help, for a weekly wage of three dollars, his food, and a new pair of boots. My husband refuses to spend any more of the money from our Colorado ranch sale. In order to cover living expenses here in town, he continues hunting, and sells the meat and hides to the settlements and forts. Josh ignores me when I ask him about the nearest ranches or farms along Beaver Creek, and how far away we will be from a school. I have a bad feeling about our new home.

1 March 1875

I received answers to the letters I had written last month to both Leticia and Mother! The children were hopping around, excited to get real letters. Mother wrote much about Pueblo, including news of Cora becoming a mother in a few months. Henry will attend Colorado School of Mines next fall, and we all are just so proud of him. Father and Mother's ranch is doing well, and Father serves on the school board. His cousins have moved on to California. Mother misses us so much, and I feel like I have let her down, with Josh moving us to Texas. But what could I do? Leticia writes that she and Mason are hoping for a better year, since last summer was so wet the crops rotted in the field. Tommy has married Maggie Smyth, a young widow from Clinton, who has a five year old daughter. Leticia says Maggie is sweet and makes Tommy very happy. The saddest news was about Amelia, since our defiant cousin returned to Bellville with a baby boy, but no husband. Of course, Leticia and Mason took them into their home. My sister is so good, just like Mother; however Leticia worries too much about me and our move to Texas. I wish I were sitting at her kitchen table right now, sharing stories about our children. I will not tell her that I am terrified about our impending move to the prairie on Beaver Creek.

20 March 1875

The children and I are alone in the rough cabin Josh built on our new land. He and George, the young ranch hand, left almost immediately after we arrived, to buy some cattle. Our journey from Cambridge took 4 days with the heavily loaded wagon, as we drove deeper into unsettled country, meeting an occasional lone rider. The second afternoon out we came upon a small ranch Josh had previously visited; the old couple invited us to stay for a meal. Mitch talked Mr. Wilson's ear off while helping with chores, and the other children chased after Mrs. Wilson's goats. Mrs. Wilson insisted on giving us half a dozen hens, which I appreciate so much; we continued toward our own place before camping for the night. A track was easy to follow the first three days, but the last day it became faint, and Josh explained it would terminate at the provisions shack of Inman's cattle ranch operation. To reach our place, Josh left the track altogether, which forced us to plunge almost three miles through the grass. The surveyor says this grass will grow so tall that by summer a man on horseback can barely see over it. The lumber wagon brought in earlier had come by a different route, so there was no sign of previous travel. What a wild, lonesome prairie this is. I now realize there are no neighbors, no school. Whatever kind of life we have here on Beaver Creek will be the one we make ourselves. The emptiness is frightening, but I cannot let the children know how I feel.

10 April 1875
Josh and George branded our cattle with the Bar B brand we chose. There is so much work to be done to mold this place into a home and ranch. Our children are thriving in this country, and I am thankful for that. I just do not know if I have the strength or desire to make an effort to work alongside Josh in this lonesome place. I do miss visiting with Marcella, and the next time Josh goes to Cambridge, I'll send a note to her.

17 April 1875
We got the roof shingled just in time before wind and rain lashed us one whole day and night. The children were so scared we all ended up on the same pallet in the night. Josh managed to find his longhorns after they scattered in the storm, and this morning he and George

took the wagon to buy more lumber from the mill. We need a shed for a milk cow and hog that he also hopes to buy. George has worked to clear a large flat plot for my vegetable garden near the creek. We got the dirt turned over again after the rain, so now Mitchell and Irene can help me plant my precious seeds. Josh is gone so much of the time, but there is no need to tell him how frightened I am to be left alone with the children. Two hands from Inman's ranch rode up yesterday. They showed us a narrow trail at the ford on Beaver Creek just below our cabin, that wanders through the tall grass to the ranch's shack, where the wranglers pick up supplies for their scattered camps. There are no women on the ranch, but about 30 men work for the owner who lives in Sherman, I believe. I am so lonely for a woman to talk to. If only Josh would show me some affection.

24 *May 1975*

My children get all the milk and butter they want now even if we don't have much else yet except wild game and corn dodgers. Last month when Josh went to Cambridge, he hunted all the way there and traded hundreds of pounds of game for the cow and a hog that will drop in about 6 weeks. He also bought a spindle-backed rocking chair. I honestly believe that Josh's feelings about me are conflicted. Not many words pass between us, but he is trying to make our ranch secure and comfortable. He has built a bed off the floor for us and trundle beds for the children. George is helping Josh clear another field, and cutting more posts to fence off my garden to keep the cattle out. Part of Inman's herd seems to like our spot on the creek. I do not know what we would do without George; he and Josh are up at dawn every day, attacking the never ending jobs on the ranch. With George helping Josh, I can concentrate on household duties, taking care of the garden, sewing, and chasing after the children. Mitchell trots right behind the men and begs to be given a job; often he is sent for a tool, or gets to hold the mules' reins.

30 June 1875

Sometimes when Josh and George take the wagon for supplies and leave our big horse, Red, at home, I pile all the children on his broad back, and lead him along the creek. We do not go far since I am constantly worried about Indians, panthers, wolves, wild cattle and snakes! Apart from teaching the children how to be cautious, I try to appear calm and sure of our situation, so they will not be afraid. The last time Josh returned from Cambridge, he brought a note from Marcella, which said she is returning to Tennessee with her son, to live with her parents. I can understand why she does not want to stay with that man, since he is very hard on the boy, but I will miss the chance to see Marcella again.

6 July 1875

For the last few weeks I kept thinking about Independence days when I was a girl. What fun we had, with friends, picnics, and dancing. I asked Josh if we could have a real celebration for the children, and he reluctantly agreed. He rode up the track to the Wilson's ranch to invite them, and two days later they arrived with a visiting lady friend. Josh met several cow hands at the turnoff for Inman's ranch and invited them to join us. George and Josh dug a pit, lined it with hot coals, and placed half of an antelope within. After topping the carcass with more coals, they covered the whole thing with sod. By the time the Wilson party and four cow hands arrived, we had opened the pit and found that juicy meat was falling off the bones. I baked several pans of corn bread, and served it with honey, a children's favorite. Mrs. Wilson and her friend Miss Burnett brought a large cake and two fruit pies. Some of the watermelons Josh planted along the far side of my garden are ripe, just in time for our party. One of the men from Inman's ranch brought his fiddle which delighted everyone. Mitchell and Irene danced for our entertainment, while Lizzie and little James Henry held hands, circling around and around. Watching the children dance reminded me of the twins, Henry and Grace, dancing at our parties back in Missouri so many years ago. Miss Burnett is an excellent waltz partner, so she was in high demand. For a middle aged spinster, she is quite sociable. Josh and I joined in a few waltzes but mostly we made sure everyone else was having a good time. Mrs. Wilson clearly enjoyed herself and we women vowed to have get-togethers more often. When the sun dipped behind the cottonwoods, we gathered around a campfire and listened to the cow hands tell tales of Indians and ghosts. One of the men, Mike, is actually just a boy who shyly listens to the thrilling stories as raptly as the rest of us. It was midnight before the cow hands headed for their own campsites by the light of a full moon. Our men bedded down in wagons and left the house for the women and children. After everyone left yesterday, I thanked Josh for such a wonderful time. It was a celebration our children will not soon forget. I can almost imagine I am happy.

30 July 1875
Mitchell just turned eight years old, and Irene is now six; I made a small cake, but did not have enough sugar for frosting.

20 August 1875
Josh is gone more than he is home. He hunts, skins, then takes the meat and hides to Belknap, Cambridge, or Sherman to sell. He is so obsessed about money even though we have several hundred

dollars hidden in the bottom of my sewing basket. The last time he went to Sherman, I asked him to bring me some calico, muslin, and denim for aprons, shirts, and pants. Mitchell went with him and I had him remind his Pa about the goods since I suspected Josh would not wish to spend the money. He has a hard time saying no to any of the children. Over the summer, Mitchell has been put in charge of the barnyard livestock. He is such a good hand, reminds me of my brother Tommy. The sow dropped a litter of nine, and soon after weaning, Josh traded four of them for supplies in Sherman. I have been making jams and chutney, and the root cellar has a good supply of onions and potatoes. We now have a smoke house George built before he left for Sherman, where he will study the law with attorney Grey. The children will miss having him read to them each evening; he is such a nice young man. Irene is my little helper in the kitchen, and she corrals James Henry and Lizzie so they do not wander off into the tall grass where Inman's wild cattle roam. Our days are so long; Josh and I get up with the dawn, seldom sitting down until it is time to eat. I usually read aloud to the family before the children's bedtime, continuing a tradition that meant so much to me as a child.

5 September 1875

Josh returned from Cambridge with a packet of letters! Mother writes that Henry has started his studies and they miss him very much since he must board at the college. Father remains active in local government issues, and Mother enjoys working with young folks at the church. Cora's letter contains 3 pages about their new daughter, Martha Ellen, named for both her grandmothers. She must be an amazing baby indeed! I so wish I could see them. Leticia's letter left me confused and worried. She only says that the situation is not good, and some questions have been asked. I can only guess that she is talking about our secret. Their farm did very well this year, so they think this might be a good time to sell out, although she will not mention anything to Mother yet. Mason agrees to move to Colorado, but not to Texas. Leticia told Tommy the real reason we all moved, and he admitted that Father had confided in him before we left for Colorado. Tommy says he plans to stay in Bellville on his farm, no matter what. Oh, how I miss my family.

15 October 1875
Josh and Mitch have taken the wagon to Fort Belknap with a load of meat to sell. On their way back Josh will buy winter supplies in Cambridge, including books and lengths of woolen fabric. I am not looking forward to a long winter here, alone most of the time with my children. I do not understand why we are living so far away from other families. Some nights when I am alone and the children are asleep, I imagine all sorts of animals and savages prowling around the cabin.

26 October 1975
A shiny new cast iron stove now takes up a large part of cabin's west wall. It is so much better than cooking over an outdoor fire, and will keep the cabin warm during the winter months. I can hardly believe that Josh spent the money for it. He must be thinking of the children.

12 April 1876
I have neglected my diary these months. We have been living on Beaver Creek over a year now. We received sad news this winter that Father passed away, and even though I wanted to go to Pueblo, I could not leave the children. Father's heart failed suddenly, without

warning. Leticia and Mason will be moving to Pueblo as soon as possible, and in the meantime Mother hired a young couple to help with the ranch while Henry is away at school. I desperately wish we could move back to Colorado. My children are well, but Josh seems to withdraw more and more.

1 October 1876

Two families have moved onto land across Beaver Creek southeast of us! The Childers and Thorn families stopped by our place while looking for a ford on the creek. Having neighbors just five miles away is very exciting. Josh is not so happy to have settlers moving in, preferring to be alone on this prairie. He forgets that even though he often travels to town, the rest of the family goes for weeks without seeing another living soul. It is up to me to see to it that our children have friends to grow up with. We desperately need a school for Beaver Creek children. I have resumed Mitch and Irene's lessons in the late mornings after chores.

1 December 1876

Mrs. Childers and Mrs. Thorn came at my invitation, so we could visit and learn about each others' families. Both ladies have three children, and brought them to visit with mine. The Thorns were born and raised in Texas, and are proud of native Texan traditions, especially of bestowing unique names to their offspring. Their son is called Smoky Jim, and the two girls are Lottie Sky and Blanca Pearl. Mitchell organized a picnic for them, with the help of Mrs. Childers' nine year old daughter, Ellen. When the ladies learned of Mitchell and Irene's schooling, they politely asked if I would recommend books for their school aged children. Mrs. Thorn confided that neither she nor her husband had much schooling, and they are determined to do better for their own children. Mrs. Childers offered to teach all of their children together. I suppose it will be difficult to lure a real teacher to this sparsely populated Texas prairie, but perhaps in time it will be possible. Mrs. Childers has invited us all to a Christmas party at their house. Actually they are living in the barn her husband built, so there is enough room for us all. Their real house, not a cabin, will be finished in the spring. Josh built a small bedroom off the back of our cabin for us. It is nice that we don't have to sleep in the main room anymore. One night a few weeks ago he quietly said he needed me, so our relations have begun again. It is very different now, an act without being fully involved.

5 January 1877

The winter has been mild so far, which is a blessing. There were twenty of us for Christmas dinner at the Childers' place, since we invited Mr. and Mrs. Wilson to visit at that time, and two of Inman's hands, young Mike and Frank the foreman. Those young men surprised the children with store bought hard candy. Two turkeys were roasted on a spit, as well as a haunch of antelope. I prepared cornbread dressing and candied yams, Mrs. Wilson baked custard pies, and Mrs. Thorn brought corn pudding and compote of dried apricots with pecans, spiced with a little whiskey. The day was great fun, with memories of past holidays when we would sing and take sleigh rides. I miss Mother so much, but having good friends helps me a lot. Josh was generous with gifts this year, a departure from his usual spending habits. Mitchell is so proud of his new hat, with the wide brim turned down in front, just like Mike's. James Henry got what he wanted: a wind-up toy train engine. Lizzie was so excited with her dolly. Irene wanted a dresser set, with comb, brush and hand mirror, so Josh chose pretty tortoise shell pieces on an oval tray. The most interesting gift of all was the one Josh got me. He has tried to teach me how to shoot his old Henry rifle, but it is just too heavy so he bought me a brand new Winchester. I suppose it is a good idea for me to be able to protect the children when Josh is away. Just last month, a Comanche family came to our place, demanding food. Thankfully Josh was home, and when he stood in the doorway, waving them away with the Henry, they left quickly.

17 March 1877

The Childers and Thorn children have been visiting back and forth with our own the last several months. Sometimes they spend two or three days at one house or another. I so enjoy having everyone underfoot. Josh has been working all month, hauling logs every day to cut and split for firewood. He says it helps clear out the woods, and we will have a head start on next winter's supply. Perhaps he is bored and needs something to do, before the real farm work begins. Our larder is in need of flour, sugar and coffee, so Josh and Mitch will ride to Cambridge, trailing a mule for the supplies. Recent rains have made the track impassable for the wagon. We bought a horse from Bob Thorn after Christmas, which has proven to be a fine animal for Mitch. Leticia writes that they finally sold the farm. They can ride the train part of the way to Pueblo, so their move will not be as difficult as when we traveled west. I wish Tommy would move his family too. Henry is excelling in his college studies, but of course he will be home to work on the ranch during the summer.

12 April 1877

The last time Josh went to Cambridge, he arranged for Mr. Krebs, who has a photography studio, to accompany him back to Beaver Creek. All our neighbors sat for family portraits, as well as several of the cow hands from Inman's ranch. Josh rode back as far as Wilson's place with him, where more photographs were arranged. The next time someone from Beaver Creek goes to town, he will fetch our photos. I am so pleased that Josh thought of this, as were our neighbors. Everyone was primped and combed; tan faces looked out from beneath the boys' slicked back hair. The girls wore new ribbons, and their best dresses; thankfully, I had sewn a new dress for myself just last month. Josh has been very attentive to the children lately, like he hangs on each one's every word.

25 April 1877

A new horse is in our corral, a beautiful bay that Josh bought from Mr. Wilson. Sandy is too unpredictable for the children to ride but Josh told me the bay suits him just right. Branding is finished, the garden looks to be a heavy producer, and game hangs in the smokehouse. At last our ranch is beginning to look like permanent part of the landscape.

17 May 1877
Josh is gone.

20 May 1877

We are alone and it is my fault. Josh left one morning a few days ago before I awoke, and left a note that said he was living a lie, and found it unbearable. He will not be back. How could I know that Josh's love was conditional? I must not break down in front of the children, so I just breathe shallow, and keep my jaws clamped to stay in control. For now, my sons and daughters just know Josh is gone. I am so frightened and do not know how we will manage, alone on this prairie.

Rosalie turned the book over on her tray, stared out into clouds enveloping the plane, and thought, "How could a father leave like that? What can Susan do besides take her family back to Colorado? Surely Josh's comment about living a lie refers to the family secret."

22 May 1877
Josh asked in his note that I tell the children he is going to California to look for gold. I suspect that is where he headed, so at least I am not lying to them completely. Mitch and Irene are so sad that Josh didn't wait until they were awake, but I know he couldn't face them. How does he think we can manage without him? For the first three days after he left, I moved through my chores in a fog, thinking he would suddenly walk through the door, having changed his mind. When I finally decided to assess my situation, I checked the bottom of my sewing basket and found all five hundred dollars of the Colorado money remained. I guess I should feel thankful. Josh must have been planning this for a long time. I now understand why he taught me to shoot, and all the fuss about putting up a huge supply of firewood; waiting until the crops were planted was to ease his conscience. The new horse must have been part of the plan, since he left Red here. I suppose the family photograph was part of it too. Last evening I walked down to the creek just at sunset, and all alone I cried until I had no more breath or tears. I thought I knew my husband so well, and to find out he had such feelings breaks my heart. I should never have told him of the secret. I need to make a plan for myself and the children. James Henry and Lizzie keep asking me when will Pa be home, but Mitch and Irene seem to sense something more serious has happened. I do not know if I can shoulder all of the responsibility that crushes me breathless when I finally lay my head on the pillow at night. Mitch found me staring off to the west one morning, looking

very sad I am sure. He took my hand and said, "Ma, I know how to take care of things, don't worry." Mitch is only ten years old, but he is my little man.

2 June 1877

It has been just two weeks since Josh left, and Clara Childers surprised me with a visit today, bringing along her three children and little Pearl Thorn. The children were happy to see their friends, and set off to catch crawfish in the creek. Mitch and Ellen worked together to fill a basket with bread slices slathered with butter and jam. Clara had some mending with her, and we sat on the bench outside the front step. I picked up the sunbonnet I was making for Lizzie, and we sat silently for a few minutes. Clara then told me that Josh had dropped by their place on his way west, telling them he had to be gone for awhile. She just came to check on us, as she assured Josh she would. I have discovered what a wonderful friend Clara is, as I confided to her the real reason Josh left, from the very beginning. At first she was shocked, I know, yet she hugged me close. We cried together, as women do, holding hands and wiping noses and eyes with limp handkerchiefs. Clara said she will die with my secret, and I know she means it. When she asked what I plan to do now, I told her I have a garden in the ground, calves to sort, children to feed and a thousand other chores to fill my days. When Clara gathered up her clan to leave, she said, "Don't forget that you have friends nearby." Perhaps later in the autumn, I will move the children to Pueblo. I am not going to write Mother or Leticia right now about Josh. I sent a message with one of Inman's cow hands, asking George if he wants some work over the summer, building fences for me.

15 June 1877

Bob Thorn returned from Cambridge today with our family portraits. Josh had paid to have ours mounted in a nice frame, so it now hangs on the wall next to the kitchen table for the children's sake. Mitch didn't comment, James Henry laughed at his own expression, and the girls vainly appraised their own poses. I looked closely at Josh's face and for the life of me I cannot see the unhappiness he wrote about.

30 July 1877

Mitch is my right hand man! He has taken seriously to his new position in the family by doing whatever I cannot make time to do. The cattle do not roam too far, thank goodness, since Mitch has to keep track of the herd when I do not have time. He tends all the livestock except for the chickens, which are Lizzie's responsibility. Irene helps me with some clothes washing and ironing. We cook the meals together, so she is becoming quite the homemaker. Our root cellar is beginning to fill with yams, onions, turnips, and cabbages. Soon I will show Irene how to make sauerkraut. The whole family gathers wild berries and fruits, like chokecherries, wild plums, and grapes. James Henry keeps water buckets filled, helps Mitch slop the hogs, and he and Lizzie weed the garden. George finished the fence I needed and has returned to town. Mike drops in about once a week, now that he is aware Josh is gone. I save up heavy jobs for his help, which he is happy to do, knowing he will be invited to supper. Some nights I am so tired, I feel that I would slap Josh if he walked through the door. How could he leave, knowing how hard we would have to work to keep the ranch running? Most likely, Josh thought I would use the money he left to arrange passage to Colorado.

21 August 1877

The children and I just returned from a trip to Cambridge for supplies. Mitch has accompanied Josh so many times that I depended on his directions. I asked Mike to stop by to feed and water the corralled livestock while we were gone. We stayed at the Wilson's place for a night, and I told them Josh had gone to California. I did not elaborate, and I am sure it left them wondering. Mrs. Wilson asked if she could come for a week in about a month, and help with the sewing I haven't the time to finish. It is a generous offer and much appreciated! In Cambridge, I traded six piglets for flour, nails, a few boards and glass window panes. George is going to ride out next week to put two more windows in the front wall of the cabin, before he is back to studying the law. About once a week I set aside time for us to spend an afternoon fishing in the creek. We have to have fun once in awhile, and occasionally the Thorn and Childers families join us.

23 September 1877

We had an Indian scare a few days ago. Mike and Frank rode up to the house warning us of a series of raids happening along the Wichita. We loaded the children in the wagon with some household items, including the land documents, and tied Red and Mitch's horse, Rob, on back. I just prayed the stock would not be killed or taken. Mike escorted us across the Beaver, to the Childers and Thorn homes since they needed to be warned, and it would be safer for us all to be together. As it happened, our properties were not attacked but a cabin south of Childers' place was burned down and a man was killed. The Indian threat is my biggest worry here on the prairie. The woman who was captured when we first crossed into Texas, was found last month and traded to the soldiers. She had been so mistreated by the Comanche that she has attempted to take her own life. That poor woman. The children and I are so relieved to see our house is intact and the animals are safe. Mrs. Wilson's visit has been delayed until the Comanche have quieted down. Inman's cow hands have been picking up mail in Cambridge for the few families in our area, which keeps me from feeling so far from Mother and Leticia. We write often nowadays, but I still have not mentioned Josh's absence. We will stay here on Beaver Creek through the winter, but I plan to sell out in the spring. Mr. Inman came out to his ranch with the winter load of supplies for his cowhands, and stopped by to see how we were getting along. He didn't know that Josh left us, and I just let him believe Josh was due back from hunting soon. Mr. Inman is actually a very nice man, and said next time he will bring his wife with him from where they live in Sherman, but I doubt she will come.

8 November 1877

Mrs. Wilson just returned home after being here for a week. We sewed up a storm, completing several full aprons and red flannel petticoats for the girls, shirts for the boys and a skirt and shirtwaist for me. I revealed more of my circumstances, but did not tell her anything except that Josh did not want to live with us any longer. She accepted that explanation with sadness and disappointment, but I assured her that we are fine, and will move back to Colorado next spring. Mike delivered an order I placed in Cambridge the last trip, for new high tops for Lizzie and Irene, and boots for the boys. Leticia writes that Mother is not well, and the doctor blames a heart condition. Amelia, who made the trip west with them, has been a great help in nursing Mother. It does sound like she has matured into a sweet young woman. I have been schooling all the children in the evenings, and need to purchase another oil lamp. Lizzie just celebrated her fifth birthday. This summer Irene begged to ride my horse by herself, astride of course, and I am so proud of her skill. She is a born horsewoman! She and Mitch make quite a pair, riding off to visit our neighbors.

15 November 1877

We are in great need of meat, so Mitch and I are going hunting. Although Mr. Thorn brought us an antelope a few weeks ago, and Clara's husband dropped by with two turkeys recently, I will not have the neighbors feeding my family when they have their own to worry about. Mitch says he will show me how his Pa looked in certain places for different animals, and how to read the tracks. We will leave the other children with Clara for a few days. I am amazed at Mitch's skill, knowing how fresh a deer hoof print is, or what kind of bird danced across a sandy hump.

2 December 1877

Our hunting trip was successful, since each of us shot an antelope, and I also got a deer. Mitch managed to shoot 3 turkeys and many quail with the old shotgun Josh left for us. Several large chunks of meat are now hanging in the smokehouse. Mitch helped me make jerky, and I offered to keep our cowhand friend, Mike, in all the milk and butter he wants if he would help us butcher a hog. There is not a real ranch house on the Inman land. Since the cow hands live in small encampments scattered around the grassy prairie, they have to cook for themselves. We always invite Mike for supper whenever he brings us the post. Using some of the hog scraps, I made sausage patties and preserved them the same way Mother did in Missouri by frying the patties first, packing the meat in crock jars, and covering it all with lard we rendered from the hog. Kept in a cool place, it will be good for several months.

26 December 1877

I was determined we would have a happy Christmas, even though the children are sad without their father here. It makes me so angry at him, for not considering just how his selfishness would affect his own children. We invited the Childers and Thorns for a big dinner, and Mike came with two more cow hands. I am very proud of my little family, holding the ranch together. The cattle have grown into a sizable herd, so I plan to sell them in the late spring, and move to Pueblo at that time. I have decided that I am glad Josh did not change his mind, and kept heading west. I could never care for him again.

20 January 1877

Mother has passed away. Leticia wrote that she died of pneumonia after being bedridden for several days. I am so sad that I was not able to see her one last time. I found it hard to break the news to Mitch, Irene, James Henry and Lizzie. I just wrote Leticia, Cora and Tommy about our abandonment by Josh. I know they will be shocked, but I assured them we will move back to Pueblo soon.

7 March 1877

All of the children have been sick with fevers and coughs. Irene has been left so weak, but the others are almost back to normal. A cousin of Clara's came to stay with them, and I believe he was sick which infected her children, and in turn, mine. Thank heavens I did not become ill. Caring for Irene day and night has left me exhausted; if I could just get a long night's rest, I feel that my body and spirit would improve greatly.

19 April 1878

George hired three cowhands to handle the branding for me this spring. Mike offered to help, but I told him he worked for Mr. Inman, and that wouldn't be fair. I told George and Mike that Josh will not be back, but I think they had guessed as much since they exchanged a brief glance. We made it through our winter alone with only the children's illness and a February blizzard that kept us house-bound for a week. Mike has been regular about fetching our post, so Leticia and I have kept up a correspondence, which means so much to me, and especially Mitch and Irene. I get an occasional letter from Rachel, who now has two children. My sweet neighbor, Clara, told me that she is expecting a baby in November.

16 June 1878

Yesterday was my birthday; I am thirty-two years old. I have seen and done much in those years, but most amazing are my children. Mitchell is eleven years old, Irene is nine, James Henry is eight and Lizzie is six. The ranch looks good this year, with many new calves born to a healthy herd. I killed several young fryers and cooked them up for a special picnic with friends and neighbors. Everyone brought food, and I think a great time was had by all. Mr. and Mrs. Wilson came, bringing a large bag of dried apples for me. I thought the children might hear from Josh this year, but there has been no word since he left. George has been here a month, attacking some brambles along the trail to the creek, and putting a new roof on the house after another bad hailstorm. I know he needs the money to help with expenses while he finishes his law studies. We all have spent many late afternoons fishing in the creek. I have cooked up several fresh catches, and smoked the rest. George is going to find someone to dig a well close to the house so we don't have to haul water up from the creek. James Henry tags along behind George all day, fetching tools and trying to be helpful. George loves it, and is very patient as he shows James how to finish off the roof. Of course, we are still here on Beaver Creek.

11 August 1878

Three families have taken up land between us and Thorns. Among them is a school teacher, Miss Tucker, who will teach all of the children along Beaver Creek. The fee is seventy-five cents per month for each child, a reasonable amount, I believe. The children and I decided that Mitch will ride Rob with James seated behind, and Irene can ride Red with Lizzie behind her, to school each day. Some days I plan to take them in the wagon, so I can visit with the neighbors. It means so much to have families moving onto the prairie nearby. I hear that there are more settlers at the falls on the Wichita. We sold part of our herd to an outfit trailing cattle to Kansas, so we have money to spare for a well digger. Mitch and I talked about Pueblo, and we pretty much agree that our ranch is just starting to show promise. With the improvements it would be a shame to leave now. I got a letter from Tommy's wife last month, announcing that they have a new baby boy. Tommy's farm is doing very well, since he has added a quarter-section to his original gift from Granny Lee. James Henry has been asking about Josh. I was honest and told him I don't think Josh will be back.

26 September 1878

We now have water right out the back door. The children even argue over who will fill the buckets. I had forgotten just how convenient pumped water could be. Next week James Henry and Lizzie will stay at the Childers' house while we take the wagon to Sherman. We are in need of all supplies, including cloth for clothing and bedding. I need to buy some geese for down pillows.

14 November 1878

Last night I was summoned to Clara's side, to help deliver her baby. I felt so helpless at times, when she struggled to stay calm while enduring so much pain. It was a long night, but a healthy son is now in her arms. Clara's husband is proud as a peacock, and named the little boy Albert, but Clara says he will be called Bertie. Ellen was quite the little mother, bustling around the room, shooing everyone out after they had a look at the new baby. Mabel Thorn is expecting a baby this spring.

1 January 1879

George rode out at Christmas to bring gifts to the children. He is taking clients in his small law office in Sherman at present. I told him I now consider him my attorney on any legal matters, and I believe he was flattered. In the spring when we go for supplies, I will meet with him to write a will. I must address what would happen to the children and ranch, in the event I died while they are young. Last month I took Irene to Sherman to see a new doctor about her eyes. He has fitted her with spectacles which she dislikes so much. Irene does admit she can see and read better.

March 1879

Lizzie was sick with whooping cough for two weeks, which frightened us all. I kept her in my room, away from the other children. It will be awhile before school re-opens since several families are ill. Mabel Thorn's new baby died yesterday from a bowel obstruction, poor little thing. Her name was Mary Sunrise. I decided to take some of the money from my sewing basket to have a barn built. A crew from Cambridge will haul the lumber out next week, and it should be up by summer.

8 June 1879

The weather is so hot and humid that my hair is out of control even in its net. I suppose I could cut off ten to twelve inches and never miss it, since it reaches to my waist when Lizzie brushes it in the evenings. Some days I pull it back in a long braid, but that seems so severe. Even wearing a bonnet, my face is so brown from all the time I spend outside, and I have noticed tiny lines around my eyes when I look in Irene's mirror. Clara suggested I rub castor oil on my face every night after washing up. Her mother swore by it, and Clara does also.

5 July 1879

A big Independence Day celebration was held in the new Wichita Falls settlement, and the children begged to go. Just about everyone along Beaver Creek caravanned over there for the festivities. There were shooting matches, a cake auction to benefit the construction of a school, dancing, a watermelon eating contest and much more. Irene would not join in the fun until Mike told her that the spectacles make her look older and very intelligent. Mr. and Mrs. Wilson came and talked of selling out to move to Sherman, where life will be easier in their old age. Mr. Green, who owns the general store in Cambridge, came to me privately and revealed he had seen Josh on a trip to California this spring. Mr. Green was on a train between Sacramento and Reno and saw Josh in the next car. He appeared to be traveling alone, so Mr. Green approached Josh only to have him rise and walk away. It was painful to hear, yet I appreciated being told that Josh is still alive. Mitchell, Irene, James Henry, Lizzie and I are surviving on our own just fine. I do not believe we will ever see Josh again, just as I do not believe we will move away from Beaver Creek. This is my home now, not Josh's, and I have come to love the prairie and possibilities for the children. Mitch and Irene would be against selling our ranch, I am sure, since their own hard work and blood are in this place. If I thought very much about it, I could cry for the life I thought we would have. Instead I am angry, and will never accept a man in my life again who doesn't respect me for who I am. The children are very happy right now, since we brought a pup home from Wichita Falls; they named him Blackie. There was a sewing machine salesman in town on Independence Day, demonstrating how well the Singer treadle model works. On impulse, I ordered one which will be delivered next month. The girls will be so surprised.

31 July 1879
Our herd is growing so fast that I decided to hire a full-time hand. Mike asked if he could take on that job, which made us all happy. He knows how we operate, and the children already consider him part of the family. Mike Stewart has been on his own since he was twelve or thirteen, when he hired on at the Inman ranch six years ago. His father was killed in an Indian attack along the Red River in the sixties. When his mother remarried, the stepfather made it plain he didn't want Mike around, so the young boy left. Mike has asked that I keep his wages for now, which I believe means he is saving up for his own ranch. Mr. Inman asked if Mike would work round-up for him when the time comes. Mike pointed out that Inman is replacing his longhorns with the new Hereford breed, something we should think about. I must admit, I want to make Beaver Creek Ranch the best in the county.

1 September 1879
I received letters from Leticia and Cora, informing me that Father and Mother's estate has been settled at last. Neither of them had

a will, which complicated the probate. Tommy, Cora, Henry and I agreed to sign over all rights to the ranch to Leticia and Mason. I was surprised at the amount of money our parents had accumulated since moving to Colorado. At present, my portion is safely deposited in a Sherman bank. Henry has completed his studies, and has taken a job as a mining engineer in Montana. He never wanted to be a rancher and is happy Leticia and Mason will keep our parents' property.

26 April 1880
Teaching occupied much of my time during the winter months, due to the loss of our teacher. I remember how Father insisted that his children have adequate schooling, and I will do what it takes to provide that for my own. Mitch insists he will be a rancher, but I told him ranchers do better if they can read and study what the experts say about cattle breeding and grazing. With more families moving into our part of the prairie, the old track from Cambridge to Beaver Creek is worn down into a passable road when it is not too muddy. Sherman is a large city, and Wichita Falls boasts several grocery and dry goods stores, a large school, and several churches. George has relocated his law practice to Wichita Falls and found a great need for his services. We can get there for supplies more often, and even plan to sell produce to the grocers, from our enlarged garden. The children work so hard at keeping the garden up that I told them I will put the money we make from that into the bank for their use only. James Henry visibly has become a more willing worker with that carrot in front of him! After he broke his wrist in December when he fell off Red, he decided to become a doctor, and says he will use his part of the vegetable money for college. I am so proud of my children, with their compassion and industry. My friend Clara is a dear and I think she hopes her Ellen and my Mitch will make a home together on

this prairie. Indeed, I agree they are drawn to each other's company when there is time for leisure in their busy days on our ranches. It seems that Clara's knowledge of my secret makes no difference in her feelings towards Mitch. Thorns have sold their ranch. Their son Smoky died in early spring after a rattlesnake bite, and they haven't the heart to stay. All of us along Beaver Creek will miss Blanca Pearl, Lottie Sky, and especially Smokey Jim, of course. The family who has taken over their ranch is from Tennessee, with six youngsters. I have not yet met them, but Clara says they are very interested in getting another teacher on Beaver Creek. With the other three families between us and the new family of Parks, there are twenty-one children to be taught. I have an idea.

19 June 1880

Amelia and her darling son Tate arrived last week. I had written her, asking if she would think about taking up the teaching position on Beaver Creek. There is no doubt that she can pass the teacher examination after the excellent education she received at Father's knee. Mr. Parks has donated a small parcel of land for the school we residents on Beaver Creek will build. It will be ready for the autumn session, with Amelia supporting herself and Tate with the salary paid by the county. Amelia is a wonder! Leticia has to be given credit for bringing out the best in the young woman. Mother must have been so proud. Following Mike's advice, I purchased ten head of Hereford cattle, and a pretty breed they are. They are built stockier, with more meat packed on shorter legs. Irene is quite the seamstress now, having mastered our sewing machine. It used to take me every evening for a whole week to stitch up a dress, and now it can be completed in a third of that time.

4 August 1880

A posse from Tascosa, up in the Llano Estacado, rode up to the ranch on the trail of a cattle rustler. None of us on Beaver Creek could help, but I offered to make a big antelope stew and pans of cornbread since they decided to rest here overnight. Mitch was very impressed with the guns worn on the men's belts.

1 October 1880

Mike keeps the ranch running efficiently; in fact I don't know what we would do without him. We lost three Herefords to tick fever, but I plan on buying more. Inman thinks they will build up immunity to the ticks over time. Mike, Mitch, and I keep detailed records of grass quality, rainfall, calving, expenses and income. The children are in school five days a week for several months, but I have Tate to keep me company. I purchased a horse and buggy for Amelia to use for her and the girls' trips to school; however, the boys prefer to ride their own horses. Our garden produced a plentiful supply of vegetables this year as it provided good meals every day, filled the cellar, and made the Wichita Falls grocers happy. The children spend many evenings looking over the ledger I keep of their bank account. I overheard Mitch talking to Mike about Josh. He explained that his pa did not love us enough to stay and work the ranch, but that his ma would never leave like that. I wanted to wrap my arms around his shoulders, and squeeze him tightly, but he would have been embarrassed. Mike replied to Mitch that he felt very lucky to work on our ranch, because I treated him like family. Oh, I could have burst out bawling! Instead I got busy making a pan of chocolate pudding with fluffy meringue on top, slightly toasted, the boys' favorite.

26 December 1880

We learned that a few weeks ago Mr. Wilson passed away. Mrs. Wilson is preparing to move to Austin to live with her younger sister. I will always remember their hospitality when we first came to this tall-grass prairie. Christmas was a happy time this year, with many friends and parties galore. Lizzie and James Henry talked me into having a taffy pulling party for all their friends in a few days, as we celebrate the New Year.

24 March 1881

The children are so excited about a new project for the family. I hired carpenters and helpers from Wichita Falls to build us a new house, using the money from Father and Mother. I just couldn't think of a better way to use it, and we really need a larger place. The bottom floor will have a parlor, large kitchen, dining room and one bedroom for me. The second floor will have four bedrooms: one for the girls, one for the boys, the largest for Amelia and Tate, and a small guest room. I want a covered porch built across the whole front and around the south side to the kitchen door. Amelia and I are looking forward to sitting out there in the evenings, sipping lemonade! The house is going to be beautiful, painted white and nestled in a grove of mulberry trees. Mike will move from his room in the barn to this little cabin, but he is already joking that it will just be more to keep clean. Sometimes, for just a moment, I wish that Josh would come back to see how we managed without him; however, the hurt he caused wipes that wish right out of my mind. I have to make certain that the children never hear the real reason Josh left.

25 July 1881

Cattle prices are up this year, so we did very well. It seems that everyone along Beaver Creek had a good year. In the spring Mitch and James Henry plowed up more prairie grass for additional garden space. About every 3 or 4 days, they load up the wagon to deliver the vegetables in town, and Irene and Lizzie tag along to keep track of the money. Leticia writes that everyone is well in Pueblo.

5 November 1881

Amelia says that James Henry is an outstanding student who challenges her knowledge in many subjects. Perhaps he will become a doctor after all. Leticia writes of her children's musical accomplishments. I remember how Tommy loved to play his fiddle, and wonder if he still does. Cora and her husband have just built a new home, more like a mansion I suppose, since his business is booming. Mike and Mitch are replacing part of the corral fence where the horses chew. There is always something to repair around here! Amelia, Irene and I have been sewing up a storm since all of us need new dresses and shirts. One of the newest families near the Park's is having a difficult winter with the father, Mr. Pierce, being sick. His wife, Nell, came over and asked if she could do our laundry every week. I welcomed the help, and am glad it will help her too. I believe she goes to a different home every day, doing laundry, cleaning and sewing, while their daughter stays with her father.

31 December 1881

This evening we all will welcome the New Year with friends and neighbors in our new house. Everyone is bringing food and Mr. Parks has a surprise for the children…fireworks! At midnight we will step outside to yell Happy New Year, when Mike and Mr. Parks light the fuses. Ellen is coming over early to help us decorate, although Amelia says it's really to see Mitch before the crowd arrives. He certainly scrambled out the door when I told him to hitch up the buckboard and drive over to the Childers place to bring Ellen back. I am so happy the children have good friends; it's all I dreamed about years ago. Some of our newer neighbors assume I am a widow, which is fine with me. Sometimes when I see the husbands and wives who live along Beaver Creek having a private conversation, I miss having a tall man by my side. Life's decisions, happy times, and worrisome winters are supposed to be shared, a natural order of things. Oh, I have had men make it plain they were interested, but what can I do? In the first place I have not met anyone I would consider coming into my home to be a father to my children. In the second place I am not sure what my marital status is. Josh has been gone almost five years with no contact. George says I can start proceedings for abandonment, but a notice would be posted in the newspapers, publicly causing embarrassment for the children. I will wait.

16 March 1882

Les Parks, a younger brother of our neighbors, has been calling on Amelia. They met at our New Years Eve party, when he was visiting family. Les has come to Texas to manage an enormous ranch near Graham, about sixty miles south of us. Amelia told him the first time he stepped out with her that she was never married to Tate's father, but it doesn't seem to matter to him. I am glad she is so happy.

15 June 1882

I hired two more hands to help Mike and Mitch get about two hundred head of our cattle to a drive headed for Kansas. James Henry wanted so much to go, but he will have to wait a few more years. The vegetable business is bigger than ever, with the grocers advertising our days to deliver in town. We hear the railroad has almost reached Wichita Falls. Perhaps one day we will ship cattle by rail from Texas, instead of driving them. Why was I so afraid of the prairie when we first came? This is such beautiful country, I could never think of living anywhere else.

11 August 1882

We have had quite a shock resulting from a letter written by a stranger. Pete Watson wrote that Josh died in the spring near Grass Valley, California, after a mining accident. Before he died, Josh asked Mr. Watson to contact us, and see to it his kit of personal effects and money was delivered to me. Mr. Watson says he will make a trip to see his own family in Oklahoma this winter, and if I agree, he will bring Josh's belongings then. Of course, I have written back to accept his offer. When I told the children, there were mixed reactions. Mitch and Irene were old enough to remember Josh before he left, and were hurt more by his abandonment than James Henry and Lizzie. Mitch just said he was glad his Pa thought of us at the end, but it was a shame he never wrote in all the years. I had to agree. James Henry took the family photograph from the wall, and commented he was happy we had this taken so we would not forget what Josh looked like. I think deep down James and Lizzie expected Josh to come back one day. Irene was very quiet, but Lizzie had questions. She asked me if her Pa left us because he was mad at her. I folded her into my arms, and assured her that it had nothing to do with her or her brothers and sister, but because he didn't love her Ma any more. I think she feels sorry for me, but a little relieved. I am mad at Josh all over again! I know one thing: I will not wear mourning. George will take care of putting the deed for the ranch in my name alone.

30 November 1882

Amelia will teach until the end of January, when she marries Les! She confides that they are so much in love, and I remember how that feeling is the greatest in the world. We have much to do to get ready for a wedding. Nell Pierce still comes over to take care of our laundry, and I do not know how I could ever get by without her. She has offered to work an extra day each week, and help with sewing Amelia's trousseau. It is hard to imagine my own daughters marrying one day. Mr. Watson wrote that he will be here after Christmas.

7 February 1883
The house seems lonely without Amelia and Tate, but she writes about their beautiful home and a number of neighbors. Mr. Watson is here now, having brought the box of Josh's belongings. There is not much of value except his watch and chain, and a ring I had never seen before. The cash is substantial though, which I will save for the children. Inside a book of *Ivanhoe* was a copy of our family photo, which Mr. Watson says Josh always kept with him. I told him I appreciated that he personally brought Josh's belongings. Pete Watson, a widower, is a surveyor by trade, and mostly works for mining companies. For the last two years before Josh died, he worked for Mr. Watson. Evidently they became close friends and shared many stories around the campfire. It seems that Josh was not sure I would still be living on Beaver Creek, since he also told Mr. Watson we might be with relatives in Colorado.

11 February 1883
Mr. Watson and I spend late evenings talking about everything! I have to tear myself away from the warm conversations, as if I have been starved for this kind of friendship. I believe Mr. Watson appreciates our quiet evenings also, after everyone else has gone to bed. He told me that Josh confided to him why he left us, and he hated himself for it. I am glad Mr. Watson knows. I invited him to stay a few

more days, and he agreed only if he could help Mike with some fence work. Each of my children hangs onto his every word, as he regales them with his many daring adventures out west. This morning he rode into Wichita Falls, and returned with new scarves for the girls, gloves for the boys and Mike, and books for everyone. When we sat in front of the fire this evening, Mr. Watson asked if I would object if he wrote to me. I brazenly asked if he would object if I responded to his letters, and we had a good laugh. It is very late now, and I cannot sleep. Am I being a silly mother of four?

14 February 1883

As Mr. Watson swung up into the saddle when it was time to leave this morning, he shyly handed me a tiny box, whispering that I should open it later. He rode away with the children chasing him down the trail. I waited until the children left for school to open my gift, and found a delicate gold brooch, shaped like a rose. How will I explain this to everyone?

20 March 1883

Our post now comes out of Wichita Falls so the children ride to town at least once a week to pick it up. They are prolific letter writers, exchanging news with their cousins, aunts, and Uncles Tommy and Henry. Yesterday Mitch brought a letter home for me from Pete Watson, so after supper we all sat in the parlor to read it. Mr. Watson wrote that from here he traveled north to Nebraska first to see his sister, and then caught the train for California. He has another year on his contract with the mining company, and after that he plans to return to Nebraska or Texas. Mr. Watson asked about the whole family, so I will answer him tonight with all our news on the ranch. We have an entrepreneur in our midst; Mike spent the winter evenings making a number of tooled leather belts to sell through the Wichita Falls Emporium. His savings account is handsome, since he lives frugally. Irene has been tutoring him in reading, writing and arithmetic, and I believe he will own a prosperous ranch one of these days.

2 May 1883

Mr. Inman brought his wife by for a visit today when he hauled a wagon load of supplies to the ranch provisions shack. He has, at last, built a rough bunkhouse for his hands. Mrs. Inman is a delicate thing, so I understand why they do not live out here; however, they accepted my invitation to stay overnight.

14 June 1883

The children and Mike surprised me with a birthday celebration! I was instructed to dress up, as did the whole family, and we girls took the buggy into Wichita Falls, with the boys following on horseback. The new hotel has a fancy restaurant, where Mike had made reservations. I feel very special indeed! A few days ago I received a small package from Mr. Watson that contained gold earbobs that match the pin I already have. Our letters come and go frequently now.

28 July 1883

Oh, my goodness, I cannot believe that Mitchell has just turned sixteen years old. He lost so much of a real childhood, having to assume so many responsibilities on the ranch. Irene, at fourteen, can run a household almost as well as I. They both talk of ranching in their futures; however, James Henry and Lizzie yearn for more citified lives.

8 August 1883

Nell's husband died of consumption last month, so she has sold their place and will return to Missouri. I already miss her warm companionship and industrious spirit. Mike suggested that I hire a married couple since we could use another ranch hand. He maintains that there is plenty of room in the old cabin for their use, and I would have another housekeeper.

2 September 1883

Buck and Bette Atherton moved into the little cabin with Mike, and seemed to be just what we needed. I was so angry when I caught Bette slipping my rose pin into her apron pocket just a few days later. Mike also said Buck had been prying into my personal business. Mike did the firing, and I got my rose pin back! The girls and I are back to doing laundry.

13 October 1883

A new teacher has come to Beaver Creek, a widow with one son who will board with the Finlay's, our newest family in the immediate area. James Henry has bounded beyond the teaching done in our one-room school, so I asked him if he wanted to attend the private boys' school just opening in Sherman. Although he would have to board there and come home only three or four times during the school year, he jumped at the opportunity. Secretly I was disappointed, since it is hard to let go of a child so young; however, I realize it is the best plan for James' future. The whole family delivered him to Sherman, dressed in our finest and stayed in lodgings overnight, so we would not embarrass James as country folk camping in our wagon. George visited us last week, which was a nice surprise. After supper we settled in the parlor with our coffee, and I found out the reason for his visit. It seems that the acreage to our east is for sale at a very attractive price. No one has lived or worked on that parcel since we have been here, and I am greatly tempted. I believe I will drive into town tomorrow to have George write up an offer to buy the three hundred and twenty acres. I cannot wait to write Pete about it. We dispensed with the Mr. and Mrs. in our letters recently, by mutual agreement. He will come for a visit as soon as his contract is completed in March.

20 October 1883

Mrs. O'Brien, our new housekeeper, moved into the small guest room upstairs today. George knew her husband, who died a few months ago. Mrs. O'Brien is a dear, sweet lady who knows hard work but has a wonderful sense of humor, and I think she will be a good addition to our houseful. Mike says one of Inman's young hands would like to work for us, so he will move into the cabin with Mike at the end of the month. My offer on the neighboring property has been accepted, so George will take care of transferring the funds. Who would have thought Susan Lee Baker would own so much land?

2 January 1884

James Henry is home for the holidays, and such a fuss is made over him. I will have to admit he looked good enough to eat when Mike brought him home. We celebrated his thirteenth birthday with a houseful of Beaver Creek friends. Such fabulous stories he tells Mitch and the girls, about living in a dormitory and enduring the teasing of upperclassmen. The report I received from his teachers is glowing, especially in mathematics and science studies. In turn, James was excited to hear all the Beaver Creek news. I purchased a small parlor piano that Lizzie is determined to play. Mrs. Cunningham, our school teacher, rides over with her boy on Saturday mornings to give Lizzie lessons. She is a lovely woman, full of laughter and kind deeds. Her son, Jesse, is five years old and idolizes Mitch, who lets Jesse tag along doing chores. Irene refuses to give up cooking duties to Mrs. O'Brien, and always bakes cakes and pies on Saturday. She sends Mrs. Cunningham home with something for the whole Finlay house where they board. Pete writes that he is very happy for me, acquiring the new property. I enjoy telling him about the plans I have for the ranch.

22 February 1884

We have been isolated for several days by a blizzard, worse than any storm we have seen. I am worried about the cattle drifting with the wind, stacking up against a bluff or rail fence to freeze to death. The small livestock are safe in the barn, even though Lizzie wanted to bring the chickens into the house. Mike and Mitch left early this morning during a break in the wind, trying to find where the cattle have gone. We had to miss fetching the post from town this week, but I know I will have two or three letters waiting for me. When we first began our correspondence, I was hesitant to reveal anything personal about myself. Pete already knew about my family secret, and that seemed enough. I finally confided that I find it difficult to trust men on a personal level, having been so hurt by Josh. In the months of continued writing, we both have opened up about our feelings and dreams, and I find that he is a wonderful listener!

24 February 1884

Mitch frostbit his toes, and Mike was nipped on his ears and nose, but they located the cattle safe in Cottonwood Canyon. The weather is warming up a little, but at one time the thermometer dipped to ten below! Mike toils into the night on his leather work as I can see his lamp burning when I cannot sleep. I have been sewing some clothes for myself. When Pete arrives, I surely do not want to look dowdy. When we took James Henry to Sherman in the fall, I bought a dainty, pale yellow bonnet to wear with my best brown dress. Now I am making a yellow and brown striped dress from a pattern I saw in Godey's Lady's Book. Lizzie wants to help so she is sewing lace on the petticoat I made last month. The whole family is getting excited about seeing Pete again.

3 April 1884

Pete stayed with us for two weeks before leaving for his new position as a county surveyor in Sherman. He will bring James Henry home at the end of the term, and can stay a week or two. I feel young again, being with Pete. We talked for hours and hours each day about our childhoods, marriages, dreams and disappointments. Pete realizes that my children are the most important part of my being. When he asked me if I had room in my life for a man, I was speechless. I said I needed some time and he agreed before kissing me lightly on the forehead. I have not been that close to a man for so many years; it was heaven. I now spend a lot of time thinking about what is best for the family. I would like to have someone to share the rest of my life, and Pete seems so sure of his feelings. He worked with Mike and Mitch before he left, when they started branding the calves. I would watch them from a distance, appreciating the respect Pete showed the younger men, acknowledging that this is their domain, and he is the guest. How could I not want him in my life? When his blue eyes seek out my own, I feel all fluttery inside, and think of how it would feel to be gathered into his arms. Pete is older than me by about ten years I believe, and somehow this makes me trust him more. His eyes were teary when he told me that his wife of five years died in childbirth, when they were in their twenties. Both of us have suffered great losses, yet we remember the sweetness of respect and tenderness.

Rosalie smiled to herself, recognizing the signs of budding love.

12 April 1884

Pete is barely in Sherman and already wrote me. He took James Henry to the hotel restaurant for a real meal that was not dormitory food. Pete reports that James is very homesick, missing his brother, sisters, and ma terribly. None of his letters reflect that, but James probably does not want to worry me. I am so thankful Pete looked in on him, and I will post a letter right away to James, with news of the ranch.

26 April 1884

Mike and Mitch are stringing barbed wire, our first, around the north pasture. It will take them several weeks to finish, but it seems like this is the future of ranching. The letters between Sherman and Beaver Creek fly back and forth. Pete wants to share his days there with me, and I with him. Some neighbors came to work on a quilt we are finishing for Clara's sister who came to live with them a few months ago. Her health is fragile, so she spends much of her time in bed. Irene asked if I would help her sew linens for her own home she would have someday. I was so surprised that my first-born daughter was already thinking of such grown up things.

23 May 1884

James Henry and Pete will be here in a week! I have been so worried about James. What a fool I was, sending him away from home so young. Pete has been picking him up on the weekends to stay in the boarding house for a break from the school grounds. James told Pete he was determined to finish the term with good grades, which makes me very proud of my son.

I had a wonderful birthday celebration, with all my children, Mike, Pete, and Clara's family. Mrs. O'Brien showed Irene how to fashion roses from frosting, for the huge cake. The afternoon climaxed with Pete's departure. His stay was too short, but we had time to talk seriously about our future together. Pete understands me so well. I have been so worried about James Henry, that it has been difficult to concentrate on myself. Pete is the kindest man I have known, with a heart of gold and passion to match. With such a full house, our only time alone was in the evenings on a walk to the creek, or when we rode out to inspect the ranch. Pete was hesitant to move beyond holding my hand or a peck on the cheek, but I longed to feel his arms around me, and more. One late evening we watched the moon rise, and when he kissed me chastely before seeing me into the house, I put my hand on his arm. For a few seconds, he looked at me, and I looked at him before he drew me into the shadows. His strong arms enveloped me gently and yet firmly, and we kissed. He leaned back and said, "Susan, I love you so much." Surprising even myself, I replied, "Pete, I love you too." Our second kiss was as passionate as I dreamed it would be. We won't see each other again until late August, since Pete has to finish surveying several large parcels of land north of Sherman. I have so much to think about now, especially wondering how the children would react if I told them I was going to marry Pete. He suggested that when I am ready, we tell them together. I have to tell someone, so Clara will be sworn to secrecy!

18 July 1884

Leticia and Cora wrote such sweet letters, after I decided to include them in my wonderful news. Leticia says she had prayed I would find a deserving man.

21 July 1884

We celebrated Mitch and Irene's birthdays together as usual. I bought a rifle in Wichita Falls for Mitch. He uses mine more than I, and at seventeen years of age he deserves his own. Ellen gave Mitch a photograph of herself, taken at a studio in Wichita Falls. Clara may be right about our two children having a future together. Fifteen year old Irene told me about the cedar lined chest that Mary Parks has, where she keeps items she is saving for her marriage one day. I ordered one through the store in Wichita Falls...the clerk told me it is called a hope chest. I have such a happy daughter as a result! I embroidered a pair of pillow cases which Irene found in the chest. Lizzie played the piano at the birthday party, making me and her piano teacher very proud. I will have to say Lizzie is quite dedicated to her music and practices every spare minute. James Henry wants to attend Beaver Creek School this fall, but says he will probably return to Sherman in a year or two. I want my son to be happy and yet get the education he needs to succeed. It will work out, I just know. Pete writes often, and I do almost every night. The ranch is doing very well, the children's vegetable business is thriving, and Mike's tooled leather goods made over the winter have already sold out. This is a busy time of the year, putting up our own vegetables and picking wild fruit and berries for preserves. The girls and I have also been sewing new clothing for the fall and winter. Pete will be here at the end of the month!

7 September 1884

Oh, my, I have so much to say! When Pete arrived at the ranch, I was waiting at the far gate so we could be alone for a few minutes. We were tempted to disappear down the trail; however, the children were anxiously awaiting our return to the house. As Pete pulled away from our embrace, he laughed that we really need to get married very soon. I laughed also, and replied that I agreed wholeheartedly! The children swarmed over him with questions, and took turns telling him about their summer exploits. After supper we all gathered in the parlor where Pete and I sat together. He took my hand and turned to Mitchell. Pete addressed my son like he is a grown man, telling Mitch that he has been the man of the family for many years. Not a breath stirred the room as Pete asked for my hand in marriage. Mitch smiled slowly, and replied he could speak for the family in giving their consent. All of a sudden the whole room broke into laughter and giggles. Mike shook Pete's hand hard and hugged me closely. Irene kissed me and confessed that none of the family was surprised at all, which caused another spell of laughter. I had not realized my feelings were so transparent. All of a sudden, Mike took Irene's hand and said this was as good a time as any to make an announcement. He was nervous, but declared that although Irene is young, they have known their hearts for some time. They wanted our blessings to be married when Irene is seventeen years old. By then, Mike said, he will have bought his own ranch. Irene was absolutely glowing as she looked up at Mike with such love in her eyes. How could I have missed that? I reached out to embrace Mike and Irene, and confessed that I had always thought of him as another son anyway. Mitchell, Lizzie and James Henry said we needed to toast the two couples, and poured all of us a glass of lemonade. Mitch asked if he could be spared the next morning to ride over and tell Ellen and her family. Clara pretended to be surprised about our engagement, but Mike and Irene's news was a shock for everyone. I feel so blessed! It has been a week since our plans were announced, and we have set our wedding date for Thanksgiving Day. Pete will take care of two small surveying jobs in Sherman and return by mid-November.

3 December 1884

Married life suits me just fine. At first I was rather surprised to see Pete next to me each morning, but became adjusted to it quickly! The wedding took place on a crisp winter day, after the scant snowfall from the previous night had melted away. All of our neighbors joined in the celebration, and George brought his new wife and the minister from Wichita Falls. My dress was a dark blue bombazine with tucks cascading from the bustle to the floor. Pete gave me an engagement present of a pearl necklace from California, so I tailored a fetching neckline to show them off. Irene talked me into buying a beautiful hat from the Montgomery Ward mail order catalog. We also bought each of the girls a ready-made dress for the first time in their lives. Pete was very emotional as he repeated his vows, which affected me deeply. I love that man more every day. Before we married, it was agreed that we would continue to live on Beaver Creek where my children are growing up. Pete wondered how my friends and family would feel about another man moving onto Josh's ranch. I reminded Pete that Josh had very little to do with the success of this ranch, and he had never lived in this house.

14 March 1885

The rain has not let up for weeks, which has rivers and streams escaping their banks and flooding low lying areas. So far our house is safe, but we have moved all the cattle to higher ground in the east pasture. The Childers are closer to Beaver Creek itself, and I hope they have not been flooded out. Mitch has been worried about them, but the creek is too dangerous to attempt a crossing. I just realized the children and I have lived on Beaver Creek for exactly ten years.

20 March 1885

Mitch finally managed to cross the creek, and found the Childers family safe. He brought Ellen back here, supposedly to help start piecing a quilt for Irene's hope chest. Actually, I believe those two are miserable when they are not together. I wonder just when they will announce their own wedding plans. Pete and I are investing in more Hereford cattle for our herd, and eventually will keep only a few longhorns as a reminder of how Beaver Creek Ranch began.

September 1885

Amelia has come for a visit so we have been reminiscing, mostly about the old days back in Missouri. Tate is a strapping youngster, a son to be proud of, and Amelia tells me that she is expecting a child in the spring. Our dear sister Leticia is now a widow. Mason died from injuries when he was gored by a bull. Her two oldest sons plan to leave for California, but M.J. will help Leticia run the ranch. Cora visits her often, and I am thankful for that. One of these days I will travel on the railroad to see my sisters. None of us had heard from Tommy for a long time until he wrote Cora he has moved his family to St. Louis. His farm is leased to a neighbor for now, while he serves as an agricultural agent for the government. Pete and I took James Henry to Sherman so he could attend a different preparatory school this year. I am determined to get there once a month for a visit with my son. Pete has found work surveying in the surrounding counties, but nothing keeps him away from home for too long. I feel as if I am as young as my own children, when it comes to being with my husband. I could blush when I think of our intimate moments. Pete makes me feel smart and beautiful, and I tell him daily how much he means to me. Our ranch prospers and we have purchased another parcel of land from a departing neighbor. The herd is a respectful size, and Pete works with Mike and Mitch, searching for improved grains for a crop to keep us diversified. Irene and Mike are so comfortable together, having been friends for such a long time before falling in love. Lizzie has blossomed as a pianist, however she will not have a teacher much longer since Mrs. Cunningham is leaving mid-year. When Lizzie is a little older, I have thought we might find a conservatory for her to attend.

3 October 1885

Pete is beside himself with joy! We are going to have a child in the spring! I had been taking precautions, but Pete is so happy that I must share his excitement.

26 December 1890

Five years have passed since I last wrote. We have a fine son named Peter Thomas Watson, adored by us and his older brothers and sisters. Mitchell and Ellen married in 1887, just as Clara predicted, and they have a little daughter named Susan. Of course that pleases me to no end. Mitch runs the ranch just like he always did, and knows most of it will be his when we are gone. They built a house on the acreage I added many years ago. Mike bought his own ranch farther west on Beaver Creek, just as he planned. Mike and Irene married in 1886 and nine months later she had twin sons. Little Michael is strong and active, but his twin brother Robert, died when he was just a month old. This last summer Irene had a healthy daughter whom they named after my little sister Grace. Lizzie studies piano at a conservatory in Dallas, and James Henry attends medical school in St. Louis. Pete and I visited Tommy and his family last fall when we decided to see James Henry off to school. After all these years my brother is still the same sweet person he was twenty years ago. Tommy and Pete talked crops and cattle for days, while I became acquainted with his darling wife and children. Last spring Pete, Peter and I journeyed to Colorado on the train, finally! Leticia and Cora welcomed us with a joyous celebration. We stayed two weeks, and talked about everything: growing up in Missouri, the war, the wagon trip west with Mother and Father, Pueblo, Beaver Creek, children and husbands. Sadly, our brother Henry died last year. No one mentioned the secret that sent our families away from Missouri and caused so much sadness when Josh left, because we know it will die with us.

That was the last of the entries. Laying the journal aside, Rosalie wondered what had happened to the family. What was Susan's secret? Rosalie hoped to get some answers on this trip by seeking her cousin's help. Mary delighted in using her genealogy searching resources to help uncover family mysteries.

Mary was intrigued with the diary's personal story and in a matter of only two days, she found documents online that revealed Susan lived to be eighty-eight, and died in her house on Beaver Creek. A county history written in the 1930's, profiled Susan as the first woman to start a ranch in that part of Texas, when the prairie was still wild and dangerous. The Federal Census of 1900 listed Pete, Susan, and Peter, along with Mitch, Ellen and four children living on the Beaver Creek Ranch. By 1920 Pete was no longer in the census and a search of the Texas Death Index revealed that he died in 1915. A search of Lizzie Baker's name revealed that she became a concert pianist; however she was a victim in the 1918 flu epidemic while on tour in New York City. Irene and Mike lived along Beaver Creek with their five children, near Susan and Pete, until 1910 when they moved to California. James Henry became a family physician and spearheaded the funding of a hospital in Sherman. The ranch is still being run by the family, Susan's great-great-grandson J. J. Baker, who descended from Mitch and Ellen.

Pete and Susan's only son together, Peter, died when he was just forty-eight, a few months after Susan's death. To find more information on his life and possibly locate some of Susan's descendants, Rosalie and Mary drove to Wichita Falls to search local records. A helpful county clerk heard them mention Peter's name and directed them to the library for archived newspaper articles. They found that he invested in the oil fields near Burkburnett, and made a fortune. Later, Peter tried to get elected to the state senate, but a threat of scandal about his family surfaced, and according to newspaper accounts, Peter committed suicide.

Being so close to the Beaver Creek Ranch, Rosalie looked in the phone book for J. J. Baker, hoping to return Susan's diary to the family. J. J.'s wife answered her call, and said he was at a neighbor's, but she would have him home by the time they arrived. Rosalie only told her they were following up on some genealogy research, and had something for the family. Following her directions, Mary and Rosalie drove through the countryside, trying to imagine how it looked in the 1870's. Cottonwood trees bordered streambeds, and pastures of tall grass were still present, just as Susan described. White-face Hereford cattle dotted the landscape, looking placid and satisfied. As they pulled up to the gate, which was hard to miss since an arched sign overhead announced "Beaver Creek Ranch, Est. 1875", a young man stepped up to open it.

"Mom said you should be here about now," and after closing the gate behind them, he hopped on his bike and raced for the house.

J. J., a tall Texan with sandy hair, and Rena, a tiny brunette, met Rosalie and Mary on the porch with friendly smiles and southwest hospitality. Their home was a modern version of a vintage Texas ranch house, and soon they all were seated in a comfortable great-room furnished with antiques. Old photos decorated every wall, and Rosalie itched to look closer. She took the diary from her bag, and when she handed it to J. J., he gasped.

Rena, concerned with his reaction, quickly asked, "What's wrong, J. J., what is it?"

Stumbling, J. J. said, "It's the diary my Great-great-grandmother Susan kept almost all her life! I knew about it, but the diary disappeared after she died."

"Who do you think had it all that time?" Rosalie asked.

"According to what my Grandfather Mitchell—Junior of course—said, everyone back then had seen Susan write in her diary, but she never let anyone read it. When she died, it went to her oldest daughter, Irene, who had moved to California by then. When Irene died in about 1950, her grandchildren packed up her old house and things were scattered. Grandfather always regretted that the journal didn't stay here on the ranch. I just can't believe I am sitting here holding it."

Rosalie nodded, "I can't remember where I found it, but maybe the person who got the diary from Irene's estate later moved to Portland, Oregon. I own a book shop there and attend lots of estate auctions, so I assume it came to me that way."

"Can I ask a personal question?" Mary said, and J. J. nodded. "Susan's youngest son, Peter, committed suicide when a family scandal came out. Do you know what that was about?"

Rosalie quickly added, "If it's too personal, please forgive us, but after reading this diary written by such a remarkable woman, I feel like a relative! As you will read, she often wrote of an undisclosed family secret."

J. J. replied, "Oh, I don't mind at all. Rena, where is that album?"

Rena excused herself, and returned a few minutes later carrying a large photo album. She squeezed between Mary and Rosalie on the sofa, and began thumbing through the pages.

J. J. explained, "About five years ago my mother got interested in researching our family trees and found an interesting document on Dad's side. At one time Susan told my grandfather, Mitch Jr., the names of her own grandfather and grandmother, Robert and Sally Mitchell, and where they lived when her mother, Martha, was born. Mom managed to locate Robert's will in Tennessee and discovered what ruined Peter's political career."

Rena opened the album to a photocopied document. Rosalie and Mary noted that it was dated in 1827, and gave each other a knowing look.

Grandmother Sally and Susan's mother, Martha, were mentioned in the will, not as his wife and child, but as *"Sally, house slave and her mulatto daughter Martha, given their freedom this day. For their devotion and companionship these years, I bequeath my name for their own."*

Rosalie breathed, "Ah ha", and Mary exclaimed "We should have guessed!"

J. J. said, "Of course, until the last few years, having any African American blood in your veins would be something you wouldn't want anyone to know. In fact, some people still feel that way. It doesn't bother me, but since we found that will, I've wondered how many ancestors knew. From what you've said, Susan knew something.

"The answer to that is in the diary," Rosalie replied with a smile. Rena proudly offered to identify the photographed subjects adorning the walls. What a beautiful woman Susan was, even as she grew older. The photo of Josh, Susan and the children revealed a handsome man surrounded by his family. Mitch looked a lot like his father, but James Henry took after Susan, as did the girls. It was easy to see from later photos that Pete, a handsome man himself, adored Susan until the last. Lizzie would have been considered a beauty by any standard, shown seated at a grand piano. When they looked at a photo of the house Susan built, Rena said it was still standing when she and J. J. married twenty years ago, but had to be torn down after a tornado damaged it beyond repair.

J. J. pointed out photos of the original cabin, still standing in the 1930's, but gone now. He told them there are descendants of other pioneering families still on the original land, just like himself. Rena added that among her ancestors was the Parks family, across Beaver Creek from Susan. Rosalie couldn't resist telling her that the Parks were mentioned in Susan's diary.

The rancher proudly boasted that each generation on the ranch has made improvements to the herd, even during the Great Depression. At present, he was collaborating with Texas A & M on a new grass hybrid. Their oldest son intends to get an agronomy degree, and plans to carry on the heritage Susan began over one hundred years ago.

As their visit ended, J. J. thanked them again for taking the trouble to bring the diary back home, and said he couldn't wait to show it to the rest of the family. Rosalie felt a sense of relief knowing the diary was in the right place after all these years. She knew that J.J. would be amazed as he read through Susan's diary; he could not begin to imagine the adventures the young woman experienced moving west after the Civil War, and on to Texas. As the two women walked along the gravel path to their car, they stopped to take in the beautiful evening that smelled like cut hay and honeysuckle with a touch of eau de Hereford. She turned to see J. J. and Rena waving to them from the porch. Waving back, Rosalie thought, "Susan, you'd be proud."

Valentines for Margaret

Mrs. Timmons, an elderly neighbor, was the last to leave. Rosalie slumped over her mother's kitchen table, thankful the long day was over. Several friends had stopped by to see if Margaret was happy with her new home across town. Rosalie's brother had flown to Portland to help move their mother, Margaret, into the Green Gardens Senior Care Home. Although Carl hadn't visited her in the last six months, he helped Rosalie and her husband, Ray, pay for care as her dementia progressed. They hired a night-time attendant, and each morning at eight o'clock, Rosalie drove Margaret to a respite care facility where she stayed until two o'clock. Rosalie, Ray, and their daughter Penny took turns then, staying with her through dinner, until the night attendant arrived. On Saturdays, Ray or Penny spent the day with Margaret and took care of restocking the fridge and cleaning. Rosalie's book store, Driftwood Books, was closed on Sundays, so she took over and usually brought her mother to their house.

Margaret had been adamant about staying in her apartment, surrounded by her own things. Finally, the time came when she needed more than a watchful eye. Rosalie's mother was very confused at first when they toured the newly built seniors' home earlier in the week, but today when lunch was served at Green Gardens, hers came on her own familiar china plate, and Margaret brightened right up.

"I sure hope she has a good night," Carl said. "Should we call the nurse?"

"The administrator told me they will call us around nine o'clock with a report. They seem to be on top of everything, getting her settled in." Rosalie responded.

They all knew Margaret would never return to this apartment, and since there was a waiting list of seniors wanting a place in the apartment building, Rosalie promised they would have everything moved out by the end of the week. Ray reminded both his wife and Carl that if they wanted anything in the apartment, it should be chosen now, before everything got boxed up and put in storage.

"Is there a chance you can stay around for a few days? We'll visit Mother tomorrow of course, and she might recognize you; every day is different," Rosalie said. Carl had been shocked when his mother thought that he was a stranger.

"I can stay through tomorrow. Why don't we knock off for today, and I'll get up early in the morning to help pack up the apartment, I promise." Carl offered.

"It's fine with me, if I have permission to roll you out of bed at seven o'clock!" Ray said, and Rosalie laughed, remembering her brother's life-long habit of resisting early calls.

"I'd like to look around and choose something of Mother's for my girls, while you two go to the nursing home." Carl said.

"You won't see her before you leave?" Rosalie asked.

"It's...uh...just so hard to see her like that. Mother was so uneasy with me today that I'm afraid I'll upset her."

"It's up to you, brother dear. Oh, I know there are a couple of things she put aside for Stacey and Phoebe," Rosalie said over her shoulder, as she went to the bureau in Margaret's bedroom. Ray said he had something in the car, and by the time he returned with a six-pack of beer, Rosalie was back with three tissue wrapped items, and handed two to Carl.

A label was stuck on each item, indicating which one was meant for each granddaughter, Carl's two, and Rosalie's daughter Penny. Through the thin tissue they could see each gift was a delicate figurine.

"A couple of years ago, Mother showed me where I would find them when the time came. I'm going to hang onto Penny's until Mother is gone," Rosalie said.

"Where did she get them? I don't remember seeing these before," Carl asked.

"When great-aunt Ruthie passed away about twenty years ago, these were left to Mother. I understand they were purchased in Paris by her husband, when he served in World War I. Occasionally Mother would set them on her dresser.

"I remember seeing them when I hooked up her bedroom television a few years back," Ray added. "She was worried then that I would knock one over so she carefully moved them to the bed. In fact, she told me Aunt Ruthie originally had four, but one was broken during a move. Margaret told me all about the sculptress, and what each figurine represented."

"You discussed figurines with your mother-in-law?" Carl laughed.

"Oh, Mother loves talking to Ray. They get along so well that sometimes I think she loves Ray more than me." Rosalie said, and they all laughed.

Ray poured three beers into tall glasses, the way Rosalie liked hers. They sat quietly, remembering the day's events.

"I miss the afternoons when Margaret could still brew a good cup of coffee, and we'd watch the news on CNN together when I'd drop by on my way home from work. She always kept up with world affairs, and definitely had an opinion on politics," Ray said.

Carl started to say something, then hesitated, and took a sip of beer while he thought about it.

"What?" Rosalie asked. "Say it, brother."

"I just, well, I wish I had a closer relationship with Mother, like you and Ray. I guess I still don't understand what made her tick," Carl admitted. "For as long as I can remember, Mother spent most of her time helping other children, like all the years she volunteered in the inner-city schools. I should have been proud, but as a child I remember feeling quite jealous that those poor children got more of her time than I did. Dad would attend my football games and track events, but Mother was always cheering on some other kid. I never understood her motivation."

"I remember as a teenager wondering why only Dad had the time to attend our open houses at school, and the plays I was in. I guess Mother figured we would understand," Rosalie said.

"I'm sure she must have been disappointed that I resented so much, the time she spent doing for others. I became kind of a pain in the neck," Carl admitted.

"Actually, after you went off to Stanford, she bragged to everyone about you." Rosalie confided.

"I never knew that. I wonder why she was the way she was?" Carl asked.

"She was a kid from the Depression, and I know that affected how she looked at life." Rosalie said.

"Lots of people had hard times then," Carl asserted.

"I know, but things like that affect different people in different ways," Rosalie responded.

"I don't even know very much about Mother's childhood, since she didn't talk about it, at least not to me." Carl said.

"I remember seeing her father, rather her step-father, only once when I was five years old, and he died not long after that. Mother said he worked so hard when she was growing up, and never got ahead. After his death, Grandmother Rose lived with her sister, Aunt Ruthie, in Florida, and I saw her only a couple of times before she passed away about ten years later," Rosalie said.

"Tell him about the trip," Ray suddenly interjected.

"Yes, well, remember when I took Mother down to a reunion in Amarillo, Texas a couple of summers ago? Afterward, we decided to drive on to Woodward, Oklahoma to see a cousin who couldn't attend the reunion. As we neared the panhandle town of Pampa, an abandoned collection of tiny houses was visible alongside the highway, easily recognizable as an old gasoline refinery housing camp. Mother suddenly took notice and announced, 'I used to live there when I was eight or nine.' I prodded her for details, but she waved her hand, as if pushing away the thoughts, and said no more," Rosalie explained.

"That's it?" Carl exclaimed.

"Have patience, dear brother. About a month after we returned to Portland, she and I visited our attorney to update her will. Later that week, Ray brought Mother by the book shop to have lunch with us, and she handed me an envelope with a copy of the will. I just put it in the little safe and forgot about it until last month when I gathered all of her important papers. I took her will out of the envelope and found several handwritten pages paper-clipped to the back."

"And what were they?" Carl asked.

"Mother wrote down some things she remembered about growing up in the Great Depression," Rosalie explained as she reached into her canvas bag. "I've made you a copy."

"Oh. Thanks, Sis. I'll read it on the flight home."

"I'd rather you read it tonight. It's very short," Rosalie said.

"Sure," Carl replied as he gave her a brotherly hug.

Ray said the beer was putting him to sleep, and declared he needed to go home. Just then, the phone rang, and they all knew it was the nurse from Green Gardens. Rosalie answered, listened, chuckled, and thanked the messenger.

"All is well. After supper, Mom refolded and rearranged the clothes in her bureau. She wanted some milk, and then went right to sleep."

Well, since Ray has his jacket on, I'll see you in the morning. I might start packing stuff before turning in. Don't forget to bring some more boxes and bubble wrap," Carl said.

Once his sister and brother-in-law were gone, Carl turned on the television to catch up on the news. After a few minutes, the newscaster began repeating himself, so Carl turned it off and called his wife, before he realized how late it was in St. Louis. Julie sleepily encouraged him to stay awhile longer.

"No," he told her, "I need to get back to the office, so I'll see you on Thursday." Carl spent the next hour packing clothes and shoes from Margaret's closet. She always loved high heels, and it appeared she kept every pair bought over the last fifty years. Surely Rosalie could find a vintage clothing shop that would appreciate Margaret's taste.

Pouring another beer, Carl plopped onto the sofa and moved the hassock closer to put up his feet. He reached for a coaster on the maple end table and saw the copy of Margaret's handwritten memories.

"Why not?" Carl said to himself as he unfolded the pages. At once, he was mesmerized with his mother's ability to recall events almost eighty years ago.

My mother, Rose, married my step-father Jake, when I was three years old. He was a rough-neck in the oil fields, following the jobs as they came up in the Texas panhandle boomtowns of Borger, Shamrock, and Pampa during the 1930's. Many times Daddy worked for fifty cents a day to pay the rent on a shotgun shack and feed an ever-increasing family. Mother was so thankful when he got a job at a gasoline refinery near Pampa, because it meant we got to live in a three-room clapboard camp house that boasted indoor plumbing. Daddy had been out of work for four months, so they had been forced to sell our old car; however, he could easily walk the half-mile to the refinery for his graveyard shift, four P.M. to midnight. A small store located near the housing camp provided the few basic goods the families could afford to buy. The owner allowed families to charge their purchases through the week, as long as they paid the bill on Fridays. This was where the school bus picked up all the camp children who attended school in Pampa four miles down the highway. I was the only school-aged child in the family at that time. Some days on the ride home from school, the bus would meet Daddy trudging towards the refinery for his shift. If he saw the bus coming in time, he'd wave with a long sweep of an arm, like he was flagging a train with the lunch bucket he carried.

Winter in the panhandle could only be described as bleak. The landscape at the edge of town was flat and brown for as far as you could see, broken only by an occasional windmill, oil rig or stand of cottonwood trees along a shallow drainage ditch or creek. The wind blew every day to some degree. During the 1930's, dust storms raged, driving grit into hair, eyes and food. My mother would hang wet sheets over windows to keep out the menace, hoping to prevent the family from getting "dust pneumonia." In the winter an occasional snow storm would hit with a biting north wind, which drifted snow across roads and piled up to the eaves on one side of a house, leaving bare ground on the other side.

I loved school, and no wonder. We were a poor family of six sharing a drafty shack, so school was a bright and happy sanctuary. My third grade teacher was Miss Wells. Women could not teach school during those years if they were married, but Miss Wells taught to support herself and her mother. She was a wonderful teacher, and made a big impression on me, especially since she believed in celebrating every holiday or special occasion with parties. Miss Wells organized the school's Halloween carnival; our class had its very own Thanksgiving feast, and we made cookie ornaments at Christmas for the tree in our classroom. For me, and lots of others, it was the only tree we had that year.

As Valentine's Day drew near, Miss Wells had each student construct a cardboard mailbox, each a work of art displaying not only the owner's name, but a considerable amount of hearts with lacy edges, and flowers of every color represented in the crayon box. These were taped to the desks' edges, ready to receive valentines from friends, to be opened at the class party on the next Friday.

Sunday before the party, I approached Daddy about buying a few real valentines. We had just finished eating one of the family's favorite dinners of boiled macaroni with canned tomatoes, accompanied by crispy cornbread baked in the big cast iron skillet. Beans with bits of bacon, or biscuits with water gravy would be on the table the remainder of the week. I planned the timing of my request when Daddy was rested and playing with my baby brother. I breathlessly blurted out that the nearby store didn't have valentines, but my best friend, Jean, told me that the dime store in Pampa had some for a penny apiece.

Daddy scratched his stubbly chin and without looking at me, he finally said, "Margaret, I don't have any money left from last week's pay, and I won't get any more till Friday." Years later, as a young adult, I recalled how his shoulders were suddenly hunched when he said those words. Now I realize he felt defeated and embarrassed. At that time, tears welled up in my eyes so I was glad that he turned away when Mother poured him more coffee. They were talking low, but I wasn't paying attention.

Suddenly Daddy turned to me and said, "Margaret, I was just thinking, if I go get my pay when the office opens Friday morning, I can walk into town and buy the valentines. If I get them to you by lunch time, will you have time to make them out before the party?"

Hugging his neck, I explained that I only needed a few valentines, and it would be easy to put the names on at lunch time, since the party was to take place during the last recess.

Mother interrupted us and said she didn't know how he could think of walking all the way to town and back, and then go to his shift in the afternoon. She also pointed out that he might get to work overtime after his Thursday night shift, and he would be too tired to do any walking. Daddy ignored her, and for the rest of the week nothing was mentioned of the party or valentines.

I was awakened abruptly on Valentine's Day by rattling doors, whistling windows, and a much colder house. Every few minutes the walls would strain against a menacing gust of wind. I knew, even before crawling over the two small sisters who shared my bed in the front room, to peek under the fluttering shade, a blizzard had roared in during the night. I also knew that it would keep Daddy from walking to town. Snow wasn't falling like we saw in our reading books, with children building snowmen in a tidy white yard. In those days, wind picked up the snow in the Dakotas and blew it straight across the flat plains to Texas, stinging and blinding as it went.

When I dressed to catch the bus, I couldn't find the long red scarf mother usually wrapped around my face on cold days, so she tied a strip of flannel across my nose and mouth and pulled her knit hat down tight over my ears. When I went out the back door, I saw that my parents' bedroom door was still closed, so I knew Daddy had heard the storm and decided to stay in bed. I wanted to stay home and miss the party, but knew better than to ask. Mother was in a particularly sour mood, already bent over the wash tub scrubbing diapers to hang over the stove.

The bus was late picking up the camp children, so the store owner let us stand inside, out of the wind. The morning at school was agonizing as I watched my classmates rush to and fro, putting valentines into friends' mail boxes. As the classroom lunch period began, students clustered into cliques to eat from their pails and sacks. Mother had spread bacon grease on a soda biscuit for my lunch, but before eating I decided I would make valentines out of a piece of construction paper for the teacher and my best friend. I had seen Miss Wells already put one in each student's box.

A soft knock drew the class's attention to the door. When Miss Wells opened it, I couldn't believe my eyes. There was Daddy, brushing snow from his coat and hat, and then unwinding my red scarf from his face. His eyebrows were crusted with ice; as he pulled off his battered felt hat, a clump of snow plopped onto the floor. Somebody behind me giggled and Miss Wells responded with a severe frown in that direction. She had met Daddy at the Thanksgiving pilgrim feast the class prepared, so she asked "Mr. McNeill, do you need to see Margaret about something?"

Daddy answered, his lips stiff with the cold, "Oh no, if you'd just give this sack to her, that'll be all, thank you, Miss Wells."

When the teacher had closed the door, she set the small brown sack on my desk, as curious classmates watched. Slightly nervous from all the attention, I opened it and peeked inside. There was a whole bundle of valentines held together by a red paper band which read 25 *Valentines for Boys and Girls*. Twenty-five! I knew I would have to hurry to print all the names on so many. I raised the lid to my desk in search of a pencil, and caught a movement through the classroom door's small window. Daddy was wrapping the scarf around his head; he saw me watching him, and returned my smile. He turned away, leaving the warm confines of the hall.

I found my stubby pencil and proceeded to sort out the valentines; the nicest one was saved to take home. Later I wrote "To Daddy Love Margaret" on the back of a colorful cut out of a Kewpie doll blowing a big kiss.

Those valentines were the last thing I got from Daddy for a long time. The years got tougher, times were leaner still. But for a man who couldn't give his family all they needed, one little girl felt very special for one day, and never forgot.

Carl carefully folded the pages, and got up from the sofa to pack them safely in his carry-on bag. Retrieving his airline ticket, he made the call to change his departure date. He needed to stay longer. His mother just had to remember him; he had so much to say.

→ THE END ←

Epilogue

Seven months later on a misty Monday, Rosalie arrived early at Driftwood Books. She removed the black wreath from the door before unlocking the bolt, and noticed someone left two boxes of books on the cobblestone sidewalk. It was common for people to leave books anonymously on her doorstep; perhaps these came from a cleaned out apartment after the death of a relative. Rosalie understood how hard it was to sort through a loved one's belongings for the final time. Her mother's death from heart failure was not expected, but perhaps easier to handle than the lingering alternative.

Penny would arrive soon to help Rosalie clean and dust after the two-week closure. The stack of mail she collected earlier from the post office would have to be opened, special orders processed, and cards of sympathy read. Rosalie scooted the boxes of donated books behind the counter, made a pot of coffee, and realized that she lacked the necessary motivation to get started. Promising herself that when Penny arrived she would jump into gear, Rosalie slumped in her chair and impatiently waited for the coffee to finish brewing. Soon, curiosity drew her attention to one of the boxes, and she lazily began removing the books one at a time, making stacks on the floor according to categories. She found two Tarzan novels that could be first editions, but without the original dust jackets, they were not worth much.

Half-way down the box, she found a small, thick, book without a title anywhere on its shiny leather cover. Flipping through the hand-written pages, Rosalie stopped to read: *March 4, 1942, Buddy left on a troop train in Oklahoma City this morning. I can't stay here in Enid without him, but don't know where to go. I heard on the radio that women can join up too, but I think I am too young. At least I am not p.g. like I thought.*

Penny burst through the door in her usual harried way, interrupting Rosalie's inspection of the wartime diary. Jumping to her feet, Rosalie waved the book at Penny, and with a wide smile she announced, "Look what I found!"

*A*va Wilson grew up in the Texas Panhandle and lived in Alaska thirty-eight years before retiring with her husband near Terrebonne, Oregon. Ava and Dan owned a rare book store in Alaska, and spent much of their time in a remote fishing village on the Kenai Peninsula. *The Driftwood Diaries* is Ava's first novel; an earlier travel article was published in Trailer Life.